Justice Is a Lie

The carnage and waste of human life was beyond anything Levi had ever faced. But he had solved the case Pinkerton sent him to solve: he knew who murdered Hiram Dawson and most importantly, he also knew why. All he had to do was to make the arrest and file the report. The trouble was, if he did his duty, he would destroy yet another innocent victim.

Ranged in front of him were six men, all armed and dangerous. Among them was the deputy sheriff and at his side cringed the killer Levi's duty required him to arrest. He knew with every fibre of his being he could not talk those six men out of resisting him. They wanted a different justice than his sense of the law would allow. Would the Pinkerton man back down and turn away from what the law demanded? There were only seconds left to make his fateful decision.

Justice Is a Lie

BILLY HALL

A Black Horse Western

ROBERT HALE · LONDON

ISBN 0 7090 7381 X

Robert Hale Limited
Clerkenwell House
Clerkenwell Green
London EC1R 0HT

Typeset by
Derek Doyle & Associates, Liverpool.
Printed and bound in Great Britain by
Antony Rowe Limited, Wiltshire

CHAPTER 1

Levi's lip curled, in spite of his best efforts. Revulsion boiled up within him. His jaw clamped until his teeth hurt.

'Why in God's name would anyone do that to decent land?' he muttered.

Spread out before him, a sick and wounded land languished in the Wyoming sun. Huge piles of black coal slag blocked the view of everything beyond. Black d st and more ugly slag covered the ground everywhere he looked. Ramshackle buildings squatted among the sterile piles of the ground's refuse.

Huge girders sprouting from some kind of equipment hovered over a small building. As Levi watched, men began pouring out of the door of that building. Though the building was scarcely twenty feet square, men kept coming and coming from within it. There would be a pause in the flow of humanity, then it would resume again. He thought more than three dozen men must have emerged before they stopped coming.

'Gotta be where they go underground,' he muttered. 'Like black ants, crawlin' outa their hole.'

That they had all been in a coal mine was obvious. Only the whites of their eyes showed anything but black. They were covered from head to toe with black dust. Dust shook from their clothes as they walked. It puffed in little black clouds when they coughed. And they all coughed. They coughed and cleared their throats and spat streams of black saliva onto the black earth. They breathed in the fresh Wyoming air in great gulps, then gasped and hacked and coughed more of the tarry phlegm from their lungs.

Within minutes, another stream of men began to emerge from the same building. Noticeably smaller than the first bunches, they walked with small, almost mincing steps. They wore much looser clothing, but just as black. Their faces, though, were markedly cleaner. Only a strip of their faces, with their eyes at its center, was covered with the ebony dust. Each had a scarf of some sort of material hanging over his shoulder.

'Chinese!' Levi muttered. 'Well, at least they got sense enough to keep their mouth and nose covered when they're in there. Didn't know there were that many Chmamen in this country, except workin' on the railroads. Musta come over here just to work in the mines.'

The line of white miners was nearly out of sight, walking purposefully toward the town of Rock Springs, perhaps half a mile away. The line of

Chinese miners walked just as purposefully, but on a different line, pointed toward the south side of the nearby town.

Levi pushed his hat back from his head and looked around. Several sidings jutted out from the main railroad track of the Union Pacific Railroad. Each siding was filled with coal cars. Perhaps half of them were already filled with coal, waiting only to be coupled together and hooked to a steam locomotive. From there they would travel anywhere in the nation that coal was needed. Much of it, he knew, would be used by the locomotives themselves.

He shook his head. Speaking to his horse, he said, 'Boy, Buck, I'll tell you one thing. I'd live on snake meat and crick water, and live under a lean-to of pine boughs before I'd crawl down in the ground like that to make a living. As a matter of fact, I don't ever intend to go under the ground at all, till someone else puts me there and pats me in the face with a shovel.'

The big buckskin gelding nickered and tossed his head as if in total agreement.

He lifted the reins to ride on when a sudden sound jerked him alert. He whirled his head in the direction the sound had come from and listened intently. He heard it again. The sound of a club contacting human flesh is unmistakable to those who have heard it before. It was followed by a grunt, then a low groan.

He hauled the reins to one side and touched the buckskin with his spurs. Already moving, as if in response to his master's mind, the horse spun and walked swiftly around one of the mountains of slag.

Less than thirty feet in front of them, a group of miners were kicking and flailing at something on the ground. One of them stood slightly back, holding a wooden pickaxe handle. The others were taking turns, as many as could reach in at once, kicking the prone figure. The one with the pick handle spoke.

'A pick handle sure stops that fancy kind o' fightin' in a hurry, don't it? Back off, boys. I'll finish 'im off with it.'

The rest hesitated, then backed up a step or two. The speaker stepped forward and lifted the hardwood handle, gripping it with both hands. The figure lying motionless on the ground moaned softly. The pick handle reached high in the air and began its descent.

The deafening roar of a shot barked unexpectedly. The pick handle splintered and flew from the suddenly stinging hands of its wielder. A tendril of smoke drifted lazily from the muzzle of Levi's .45.

As if pulled by a single string, all eyes spun to rivet on the intruder. Silence hung like a curtain of death, draped suddenly over the would-be party.

One of the miners found his voice. 'Who're you? Whatd'ya think you're doin'?'

A murmur of voices gave assent to his outrage. The wielder of the pick handle glared in silence, rubbing his hands, trying to shake the stinging numbness from them.

Levi's voice was deceptively calm. 'You boys must sorta dislike that fella on the ground, huh?'

The eyes of the miners darted to their prone victim, then back to Levi. The one who had spoken continued to speak for the rest. 'Why wouldn't we? Him an' all them rat-eatin' pagans like 'im. They oughta all be run·outa the country. All they do is come over here an' take our jobs. Soon's they get enough money, they hightail it back to China, takin' our money with 'em, while our families go hungry. Along with whatever they can steal. Then they smoke their opium an' live like kings over there the rest o' their lives, on the money they done us outa.'

'He's a Chinaman?'

'O' course he's a Chink. He'd be a good un by now, if you hadn't stopped us. Now get outa here an' let us finish what we got started. We're fixin' to send a message to the UP an' to all them slant-eyed devils, that we're all done givin' up the good rooms in the mine, so's they kin have 'em. Now go on. Git! An' forgit anythin' you seen here, if'n you know what's good fer ya.'

The others nodded in agreement. Levi shook his head.

'Naw, I guess not. I got too much man in me to let a bunch of grown men keep on kickin' a man that's down till they kill 'im. You made your point. Now you best get on over to the saloon and warsh that coal dust outa your throats, and slap each other on the back and tell each other how tough you are, to all together whip up on one Chinaman.'

9

Almost as one the group swung to look at the man from whose hands Levi had shot the pickaxe handle. He continued to rub his hands as he glared at Levi.

'Who are you?' he demanded.

Levi shrugged. 'Like I said, just someone with too much man in 'im to stomach what you're doin'. Now you boys best get movin'.'

'You ain't got bullets enough left in that hogleg to kill us all,' the miner argued.

'That's a fact,' Levi agreed at once. 'But I got five left. That's enough for all but one of you, and I can kill those five before any of you can take one full step toward me. That'll only leave me one to have to deal with, and I ain't layin' on the ground, an' you don't have your pick handle any more. Now I'm gettin' real tired o' talkin'. You boys gonna find out which five die and which one gets whipped, or you gonna get movin'?'

Six men glared holes in him for several heart-beats. Then the first speaker said, 'Let's go. We made our point. Ain't worth gettin' shot over.'

He turned and began to walk away. Immediately the others moved after him. The pick-handle wielder was last to go.

'You best leave town, stranger,' he advised. 'Your life ain't worth no more'n his if you stick around this town. We don't like Chink-lovers here.'

Levi didn't bother to answer as the man hurried after his fellows. Instead he holstered his gun and swung out of the saddle. He squatted beside the prone figure, who was still moaning. 'Can you hear

10

me at all?' he asked quietly. 'They're gone. If you can hear me, you need to open your eyes.'

After only a second's hesitation, the man's eyes opened. Darting this way and that, they came to rest on Levi.

'You chase them away?' he wheezed.

Levi nodded. 'They were about to kill you.'

'I thought I dead,' the Chinaman agreed.

'Can you get up?'

'Not know. I tly. Maybe help?'

Sliding his hands into the man's armpits, Levi lifted the man onto his feet. He stood there, swaying back and forth. 'Not walk much, I think. Maybe go tell honoled father come help me.'

Levi shook his head. 'I don't 'spect that's a good idea. Soon as I leave, your friends'll likely come runnin' back. Can you get on my horse without passin' out?'

'I not lide horse, ever.'

'Well, I guess this is your day to start. You ain't gonna get far tryin' to walk. Here, stick your foot in the stirrup, right here.'

With a Herculean effort against the pain that radiated through him, the young man managed to get his foot into the stirrup.

'Now, step on up into the saddle. I'll help you, as best I can.'

As Levi said it, he gathered a fistful of the loose fabric at the seat of the man's pants and lifted. The Chinaman uttered a stifled yell as he swung up into the saddle. He sat there, gripping the saddle horn with both hands, swaying back and forth.

Even his lips were white, made more vividly so by the contrast with the black dust that covered him.

'Now git your foot outa the stirrup,' Levi ordered. 'I gotta git up too.'

The young man moved his foot out of the stirrup. Levi slid his booted toe into it and swung easily into the saddle. He squeezed down between the bedroll and other things tied behind the saddle, and the Chinaman's slender body in front of him.

'You ain't no bigger'n a kid,' he said. 'What are you doin' workin' in a mine.'

The young man did not answer. He resolutely gripped the saddle horn. A groan escaped through his tightly gritted teeth.

'Walk easy, Buck,' Levi ordered his horse. 'Let's see if we can find out where this young sprout lives.'

They were nearly to the outskirts of Rock Springs when two men, obviously Chinese, appeared, walking hurriedly toward them. As they approached, they gestured toward Levi and began to speak animatedly.

Levi stopped and waited for their approach. When they stopped before him, he said, 'You fellas speak English?'

'Speak English all wely good,' one of them replied.

'You lookin' for this fella?'

They both nodded. 'You beat him up bad.'

Levi shook his head. 'No. There was half a dozen beatin' on 'im. I sorta stopped the party.'

They looked at each other in confusion. They spoke back and forth in a musical sing-song language. The young man in front of Levi stirred. He spoke to them, slurring his words, in the same sing-song cadence.

The two men in the road bobbed their heads rapidly. 'Ah, you fliend. You help Tang. You bling Tang home, honolable father's house. Yes?'

Levi nodded. 'You lead the way. I'll try to keep 'im in the saddle till we get there.'

The two hurried off, with Levi's gelding matching himself to their pace. In less than ten minutes they crossed a bridge across Bitter Creek and entered a sprawling town of shacks and tents. They stopped in front of a more substantial structure. Above the door a sign announced its purpose to those who could read the writing. It announced nothing at all to Levi.

'This where his family lives?' Levi asked.

The man who had spoken before nodded. As he started to speak, another Chinese man, perhaps forty years old, hurried out of the door. A cry of alarm keened out of him as he hurried to the horse, holding up his hands. The young man reached for him, falling into his arms. The one who had reached for him and one of the others grabbed him and carried him through the door. The other one stayed to speak to Levi.

'Was vely much good thing you do,' he said. 'Is double plenty much for you, now I think. You save Tang Lu's life, he tell us. His honolable father, Sun Lu, own store. He make you plenty, plenty, uh, thank, uh, money, maybe, save his son.'

'I don't need any thanks,' Levi declined. 'I just hope the boy makes it.'

'Makes it? What means, "makes it?" '

'I hope he lives. I hope he gets OK.'

'Ah, yes. Yes. We wely, uh, oblige to you. My name, My Chin. May I know you name, ally same?'

'I'm Levi Hill. Tell your young friend not to get separated from the rest of you next time.'

'Ah, yes. Yes. We know that ally much. We keep togethel. But we not know he not with us until we home, and Sun Lu come to say, "Whele is my son?" Then we hully back there, but too late if you not be thele to save him. Now the ones who wish to kill Sun Lu will wish to kill you, ally same.'

'Yeah, I 'spect. It's not the first time folks have wanted that.'

The chill that tingled its way up his back said this time he had made more enemies than he could fight. That shiver kept running up and down his spine as he turned and headed back across the bridge toward Rock Springs.

CHAPTER 2

'You the sheriff?'

J.C. Watkins looked up from the papers on his desk. 'Deputy Sheriff's in Green River. How can I help you?'

'Name's Levi Hill.'

Watkins's eyebrows shot up. 'The Pinkerton?'

Levi nodded.

'What brings Pinkerton to Rock Springs?'

'Workin' on a murder. Pertneart got in on another one, ridin' in.'

'That so? Somebody try to kill someone?'

'Half a dozen somebodies. They had a young Chinaman down, kicking the stuffing out of him. Fella with a pick handle was about to finish him off, when I rodc up.'

Watkins sighed. He leaned back in his chair, making it squeak loudly. 'You bought in?'

Levi nodded again. He chuckled suddenly. 'I sorta shot the pick handle out of the guy's hands. He was a little bit surprised. Hadn't heard me ride up.'

Watkins chuckled as well, at the mental image. 'That'd be a surprise all right. His hands'll tingle an' hurt all night, most likely. I had somethin' sorta like that happen to me onct. I was fixin' to shoot my rifle, in the war, an' a round hit my rifle butt. Shattered the stock, an' knocked it outa my hands. It was the god-awfullest feelin' I ever had. My hand and arm kept hurtin' and stingin' fer pertneart a week. I thought it tore my shoulder off for a while.'

'He was rubbing his hands some all right,' Levi agreed. 'Wasn't too happy.'

'I take it they left without killin' the Chinaman?'

'Yeah, they decided it'd be a good idea. I hauled the Chinaman on home. His people was comin' lookin' for him before I got him over to China Town.'

'Hong Kong.'

'What's Hong Kong?'

'China Town. It's called Hong Kong, here. Everything south o' the crick. They was comin' lookin' fer 'im?'

'They'd decided he didn't make it home with 'em, so they were coming back to find him.'

'Find out his name?'

'Tang Lu.'

'Tang Lu? You don't say! His dad owns a store over in Hong Kong. His uncle runs a laundry. One o' the big families among the Chinese.'

'I met his dad. Sun Lu, I think his name is.'

'That's him. That woulda blowed the lid off o' things, if they'da kilt him. Not that it ain't gonna blow off one o' these days anyway.'

'There seems to be a lot of hard feelings between the white miners and the Chinese.'

'That's one way o' puttin' it. They hate each others' guts, is more accurate. With good reason, from the white side, I'd say.'

'That so?'

'The railroad's to blame. They bring the Chinese in to work the mines. 'Most every white man that works in there does it 'cause they can't find no other work. That means they ain't got nothin', not even money to git the stuff they need to start workin'. So the railroad sells it all to 'em. Company store. Puts it on their tab. Takes it outa their wages. Charges the white men three times what they charge the Chinese.'

'Why do they do that?'

'Tryin' to freeze the white miners out. The white miners have organized a union. Chinese won't join it. Chinese work cheaper, longer hours, less money. So the railroad gives the Chinese the rooms in the mine that got the most coal, that's easiest to get at. That way they make more. The boys got good reason to be sore. The trouble is, they're sore at the Chinese. They oughta be sore at the Union Pacific. They're the ones behind it.'

'Sounds like a recipe for trouble.'

'Dang right it is. An' I'm gonna get stuck smack dab in the middle of it, sure's anythin'. Did you get a good look at the boys tryin' to kill Tang?'

'Yeah.'

'Can ya gimme a description?'

'Sure. They were all dressed in black, head to toe. Faces were all black. Hands were all black. Shouldn't be too hard to find six all black men amongst a town full o' whites.'

Watkins chuckled. 'Yeah, that'll be easy enough. I'll jist saunter out among 'em an' look fer fellas what's all black. Shouldn't have more'n a thousand er so to sort out. Whose murder you s'posed to be workin' on?'

'Hiram Dawson.'

Watkins made a noble effort to avoid any expression. His eyes narrowed slightly. His lips tightened. The muscle at the hinge of his jaw bulged once.

'Dawson, huh?'

'You knew him?'

Watkins nodded. 'I knew him. His brother an' him was partners in the mercantile store up town.'

'That so? I didn't know he had a brother here.'

'He does. Couple o' girls, too.'

'Who does, Dawson or his brother?'

'They're both Dawson. The dead one.'

'No wife?'

'Nope. She up an' died, four, five years ago. Left 'im the two girls.'

'How old are they?'

'Oh, the oldest is prob'ly eighteen er so. Other'n is maybe fifteen, sixteen.'

'They still here?'

'Oh, yeah. They live in the house yet. Randolph looks after 'em.'

'Randolph?'

'Dawson. Hiram's brother.'

'Were you here when he was killed?'

'Yup.'

'You investigated it?'

'Yup.'

Silence hung heavily in the office as Levi waited for more information. When none was forthcoming, he began to prod. 'Well? Did you dig up any leads?'

Watkins shrugged. 'He was shotgunned. Died straight away. Some o' the Chinese, most likely.'

'Why them?'

'Well, like I said, the UP charges white men three times as much as they do the Chinks for stuff. Hiram an' Randolph was tryin' to balance the odds a tad. They'd sell white miners what they needed jist as cheap as the UP would sell it to the Chinks. They'd also run 'em a tab, fer a month er so. That way they could get started, without goin' in hock to the company store so deep they couldn't never catch up. The Chinese didn't like it none. That took away their edge. So I 'spect they picked somebody to slip over an' gun 'im down, to try to stop 'em o' doin' it.'

'Did you talk to any of the Chinese about it?'

Watkins snorted. 'You kiddin'? You ever try gettin' any information outa them? Even if you're tryin' to help 'em, they ain't gonna tell ya nothin'.' His voice took on a high-pitched sing-song, in imitation of the Chinese. ' "Not know nothing ally same. Not see nothing, ally same. Not have ally same information." You ever notice how they use an 'l' every time they's an 'r' in a word. I can't even pernounce it, the way they do. Sounds dumber'n dumb. No, I didn't even bother askin' 'em nothin'. No sense wastin' my time. No sense you wastin' yours er Pinkerton's, either. Kilt by Chinese person or persons unknown. End o' the story.'

Levi scowled in silence for a long moment. Finally he said, 'Were there any Chinese in particular he's had words with?'

'Yeah. A couple. Fella by the name o' Wang Chou is most likely the one. He's the one that come an' talked to Dawson a couple times. Wanted the same break on stuff for the Chinese that they was givin' the white miners.'

'Did they give it to them?'

Watkins snorted. 'You sure like makin' jokes, don't ya? Course not! That's the whole point. They're tryin' to even the playin' field some, 'cause the UP tilts everything to the Chinks. It'd defeat the purpose if they did the same fer them.'

'Has the railroad had a problem with it?'

Watkins pursed his lips. 'Now there's an angle I hadn't thought of. I s'pose maybe the railroad coulda hired somebody to do it. Yeah, they was plumb bent outa shape about it too. They sent a couple company big shots, even, to talk 'em outa what they was doin'. That got a bit heated too, I guess. Dawson kicked 'em outa his store.'

'So you think the railroad could have hired somebody to get rid of him?'

'Possibility, I s'pose. My money's still on the Chinks, though. Either way, your chances o' findin' out who pulled the trigger are somewheres betwixt slim an' none.'

'Yeah, well, I'm sorta used to that. There a good place in town to stay?'

'Fer the night?'

'For however long I end up stayin'.'

'No call for ya to stay. Like I said, you ain't gonna find out nothin'.'

'I still got a job to do.'

Watkins eyed Levi carefully. He cleared his throat. 'Look, Hill. Lemme make ya a suggestion. One lawman to another. It'd just be best all around if you was to write out a report what says what my investigation already found out, an' let it go at that. Some things is better just left alone.'

'Why is that?'

Watkins looked uncomfortable. 'Just are. You've known some like that, if I ain't mistook. Part o' bein' a law officer is knowin' when to push, and when to back off. This here's one o' them times I'm suggestin' would be good for you to back off.'

'You sayin' you don't want me investigating this murder?'

Watkins held up both hands. 'No, no. I ain't sayin' no such thing. Investigate till hell freezes over, fer all I care. I'm just offerin' a bit o' friendly advice. It's a dead-end road. You ain't gonna find nothin'. Who hired Pinkerton anyway?'

'Not my job to know or to ask,' Levi responded. 'I take my orders from Pinkerton. I 'spect he has family back East or somethin'. Anyway, thanks for the advice. I'll be makin' up my own mind. There a good place in town to stay?'

Watkins sighed heavily. He waved a hand dismissively toward the town.

'Ma Corder's. Go down Front Street here to the third corner. Fourth house north on the east side. Don't take no miners, so you don't hafts keep shakin' coal dust outs your clothes. She feeds her boarders too, an' it's a sight better grub than you kin get at either café.'

'Much obliged. I 'spect I'll be seein' you around town for a spell.'

'If you go diggin' too hard, I 'spect I'll be seein' you, all right enough. Laid out at Ollie's.'

'Ollie's?'

'Oliver Earlewine. He's our undertaker. Coffins an' fine furniture. Right down the street. Good carpenter. Fair to middlin' undertaker. Course, I ain't heard none o' his customers complain about that neither, now that I think about it.'

'Good to know.' Levi smiled as he left the office. 'Always nice to know I'll be in good hands if I need his services.'

The knot in his stomach assured him that just might be a possibility. There were already six men in town ready to bring that about, he was sure. How many more would there be by the time he was finished with this business?

A vision of open spaces appeared suddenly in his mind. Tall mountains and big sky loomed high and clean and free. He looked around him at the bustle of activity along the dirty street. Coal-dust mixed with the light-brown soil. No blade of green grass in sight. No bright bloom of wildflower. Only congestion and dirt and people and waiting death. He allowed himself one long stare into the picture in his mind. Then he nudged his horse down Front Street, third corner, turn north, third house on the east.

CHAPTER 3

The bell suspended from the top of the door jingled brightly. Levi stepped into the dim interior of the store.

'May I help you?'

He started to answer, then caught his breath. Words fled. A stunningly beautiful face filled his vision. Dark, nearly black hair fell in soft curls to shoulders slightly broad for a woman. The hair framed a face he thought perfect in every detail. Eyes of brilliant blue were captivatingly out of place with the dark color of the hair. The slight downward curve of her nose swept gently upward at its tip, giving it just the slightest hint of impudence. A bridge of faint freckles danced across her cheeks and across the bridge of the nose. Full, red lips curved upward in a polite but reserved smile. The eyes danced and twinkled at his obvious discomfiture.

Almost against his will, his eyes traveled from her

flawless face down to her high-button shoes, then back again. The rest of her was as flawless as the face.

He found his voice with a rush. 'If your name happens to be Helen, I think a thousand ships would be too small a fleet.'

She giggled unexpectedly. 'Well, I must say, that certainly beats the usual "Uh, gosh, ma'am, uh, I forgot what I wanted." '

He laughed with her. 'You haven't asked me if I forgot what I came in for.'

'Oh, and did you forget?'

'I don't remember.'

She giggled again. 'At least you're not illiterate. Have you read Homer?'

'A couple or three times. Been a long time, though.'

'That's amazing. I don't meet too many people out here that have.'

'It might surprise you. Folks don't flaunt their education much out here.'

'And do you?'

'Well, I didn't need to ask what an "apothecary shop" was.'

'Then I assume you came in for something in particular?'

'As a matter of fact, I did. I was hoping you might have a balm that would heal up my hands. They've gotten awfully chapped.'

He held out his hands as he spoke. The backs of both were red and rough. Cracks in the skin gapped sorely.

'Oh, my goodness!' she said. 'They really are. I

think some petro-carbo salve would help them a lot.'

'What's it got in it?'

'Aha! Now you start talking like a cowboy. "What's it got in it?" Don't you mean, "What does it have in it?" '

He grinned. 'Yes, ma'am, Miss Teacher, ma'am. Do you want I should oughta go stood in the corner now?'

She giggled again in response. He had to admit he loved the sound of that giggle.

'No, but I may make you wear a dunce cap if you do it again.'

'Are you married?' he asked abruptly.

Her smile disappeared instantly.

'No, why?'

'Spoken for?'

'No. Why?'

'Well, I was about to ask if I could take you to supper, but I didn't want to be out of line.'

'That would be out of line in any case. I don't know your name, nor do you know mine. We are total strangers.'

'That's a fact. My name's Levi Hill. And yours?'

'I'm Sarah Miles.'

'You own this store?'

'No, of course not! It's my father's store.'

'And your parent' name? Other than Mr and Mrs Miles, that is.'

Her giggle returned. 'Jonathan R. and Henrietta M. Miles, Mr Hill.'

'OK, Miss Sarah Miles, daughter of Jonathan and Henrietta Miles, may I have the pleasure of your company at supper, since we are no longer strangers?'

She flushed suddenly, but whether from embarrassment or anger he couldn't tell.

'So that's what was behind the questions. Well, Mr Hill, it won't work. On the other hand, if you come back tomorrow and ask again, I just might change my mind.'

'Fair enough,' he said. 'Now, how about that balm.'

'Salve.'

'What's the difference?'

'Balm sounds so – so – I don't know. Stuffy. Biblical, maybe. Balm of Gilead, or something like that.'

'But there is no balm in Gilead, the Lord says. Hey, isn't this stuff for cow's, uh, I mean, uh, well. . . ?'

She giggled again. 'You can say the word, Mr Hill. Yes, it's made for chapped cows'-teats. Or tits, as all the cowboys say. But it's the best salve for chapped hands I've ever found. It'll have your hands healed up in three or four days. Rub it in good night and morning.'

'How much?'

'Fifty cents.'

'High priced stuff. It oughta be good.'

'Money back if not completely satisfied.'

'Well, I'll come in tomorrow to complain. That'll give me an excuse.'

'What do you do, Mr Hill?'

'Levi,' he corrected her. 'I'm a detective for

Pinkerton Detective Agency.'

'Are you after outlaws here?'

'I'm investigating a murder.'

She sighed. 'Well, it isn't as if there aren't enough of them to investigate. There'll be even more one of these days, I'm afraid. Whose murder are you investigating?'

'Hiram Dawson.'

A small gasp escaped her lips before she clamped them shut.

'You know him?' Levi pursued.

'I knew him, of course,' she said. 'He was a fine, upstanding member of the town's business community. He and his brother owned the mercantile store.'

'So I understand. You know his daughters?'

'Lily is my very good friend. My mother has been something of a surrogate mother for her and Adelia, I guess, since their mother died.'

'His murder must have been hard for you too. Any idea who killed him?'

Her voice was harder, her words more tightly clipped as she responded. 'I have no idea why anybody would want to harm Hiram. He was a good man. He was totally devoted to Lily and Addie. They think some of the Chinese were angry that the Dawsons were selling miners' supplies to the white men more cheaply than the railroad would sell them. They don't treat the Chinese and the white miners the same, you know.'

'So I've heard.'

'You might spend your time more productively investigating the railroad, and forget about poor Hiram's murder.'

'You're the second person that told me that today. Any particular reason you don't want me investigating Hiram's murder?'

'No! I didn't say that at all. I wish you wouldn't, though. Poor Lily's been through enough already. Opening up those wounds isn't going to help her a bit.'

'I 'spect it'll be a bit tough on her,' he agreed. 'I'll try to be as easy on her as I can.'

'I would personally appreciate that,' Sarah said. 'She's a really fine person. Where are you staying in town?'

'Ma Corder's. By the way, thanks for reminding me. I 'spect I oughta mention it if I'm likely to have a guest for supper tomorrow. I'm told her food is better than any of the local cafés'. So just for her benefit, may I tell her you're likely to be my guest at supper tomorrow?'

Sarah's pleasant giggle returned like a breath of springtime to Levi.

'Now that's a roundabout way to ask a girl to supper if I ever heard one! Yes, Mr Hill, if you promise to be very careful of Lily's feelings while you investigate, I will accept your offer of supper tomorrow. Providing you stop in tomorrow and ask, of course.'

'Of course. Wild horses couldn't keep me away.'

The town seemed strangely less confining and foreboding as he walked back to the boarding-house. The can of petro-carbo udder-and-teat salve dangled in a paper bag from his left hand.

CHAPTER 4

The Pastime saloon lived up to its name. Miners, mostly, passed the time they were not delving beneath the ground in its almost equally dim interior. 'Must be used to livin' in half-light,' Levi muttered to himself.

The Pioneer saloon down Front Street was much more to his tastes. Though not a drinking man, he spent a lot of time in saloons. It was there the pulse of a town could be felt. It was there the gossip-mills ground reputations into fine dust or built them into hero status. It was there that whiskey-loosened tongues often let slip a word that led him to his quarry.

The Pioneer was patronized mostly by the cowboys and ranchers, the homesteaders and the drifters. It was almost as if those who toiled beneath the earth were of some different race, unwelcome in the world of sunshine and rain.

Levi shared the feeling. Pertneart like crawling under the ground to walk in here, he thought.

There were differences other than the dimmer

lights. Trouble crouched always ready to spring in either saloon. The biggest difference was the underlying sense of the trouble. In the Pioneer, the mood was usually bawdy and boisterous. Conversation bubbled and ricocheted off the walls. Comments were yelled from one side of the room to someone at the other side. There was a free sense of untamed wildness in the place. That wildness could break out into conflict at any moment, but it did so openly. It was announced. It was challenged. Challenges were accepted exuberantly.

The mood of the Pastime was darker, brooding, subdued. Conversation growled in surly tones. Some heavy, somber undertone seemed to pull voices down an octave deeper. It stirred its way around the room like the turgid tide at the bed of some deep river.

Even the 'working girls' seemed different. At the Pioneer they laughed a bit too loud, flirted too brazenly, and plied their ancient trade with relish and abandon. When a cowboy would engage the services of one of the girls, she would usually lead him from the room by his neckerchief, often to the taunts and jibes of his fellows.

At the Pastime, the girls laughed at the patrons' crude jokes, but there was a hard, almost stifled note in the laughter that scarcely carried to the next table. When they were 'hired' they slunk quietly out of the room into the deeper darkness of the adjoining hallway. At their elbow, their 'customer' followed in silence. Nobody offered any comment, or even seemed to notice or care.

It took a while for Levi to figure out the difference that grated most on his nerves. At the Pastime, there was a background noise of almost constant coughing, clearing of throats, and blowing of noses. The sawdust that covered the floor was black in a circle around every table, where coal dust, broken loose from the walls of lungs, was hacked up and spit into the sawdust.

Levi stopped at the bar. His high-crowned, broad-brimmed hat was as out of place there as his booted feet and leather vest.

'Beer,' he told the bartender.

The bartender hesitated for a brief instant, then almost imperceptibly shrugged his shoulders. He sat the beer on the bar in front of Levi and took his coin. Levi carried it to an empty table against the back wall, and sat down to watch and listen.

Within twenty minutes the undertone of the conversation subtly changed. Furtive glances began to stab in Levi's direction, then divert hurriedly.

From a nearby table, a giant of a man slowly rose to his feet. He glared in Levi's direction, then walked across the intervening space. In spite of his size he moved smoothly. Like a big cat, Levi thought, watching him approach. There is a dangerous man.

He sat down across from Levi, giving the impression that he was relaxed, but his weight remained balanced on the balls of his feet.

'Who're you?' the big man demanded.

'Happy to meet you, too,' Levi responded

evenly. 'My name's Levi Hill. Sorry, I guess I didn't catch yours.'

'I didn't say it.'

'Oh. Well, that's probably why I didn't hear it. You got one, or do folks mostly just make up one for you?'

'One what?'

'Name.'

'Yeah, I got a name.'

'Well, good. That's a relief. I'm plumb outa spare names, and I thought I was going to have to come up with one for you. But since you already have one, I won't have to do that. What name is it that you've already got?'

The big man blinked rapidly in the gloom. He hesitated for several seconds, then finally came to a decision.

'Luke,' he growled. 'Luke Wright. What d'you want in here?'

'Well, at the moment, I was drinking a beer.'

'No you ain't,' Luke argued. 'You been holdin' that same beer since you come in. You look a whole lot more like a cowboy than a miner. The cowboys got their own saloon down the street. What you doin' in this one?'

'Just looking for some of this great conversation,' Levi quipped. 'Cowboys, they just don't have a grasp of the language like miners have.'

Luke frowned in confusion. 'What's that supposed to mean?'

Levi waved a hand. 'Nothing. What can I do for you, Luke Wright?'

'You can tell me what you're doin' here,' the miner insisted. 'You come to town lookin' for somethin'?'

'Well, if I did, I wouldn't hardly announce it, now would I?'

'You work in' for the railroad?'

'Nope. I got no love for the railroad. I haven't seen them do much but cause a whole lot of problems.'

'You workin' for them rat-eaters?'

'Nope.'

'Then how come you're fightin' their fight?'

'I didn't know I was.'

'You're the cowboy what butted into a fight yesterday, ain't ya?'

'I don't remember any fight. I do seem to remember six husky miners beating the stuffing out of a Chinese kid about half the size of the smallest one. Are those Chinese fellas really tough enough that it takes six of you miners to whip one of 'em?'

Even in the dim light Levi could see the color darken in Luke's face.

'You bought into somethin' that ain't any o' your business,' he growled.

'It's always my business when I see a helpless man about to be murdered. I don't remember seeing you there, though, Luke. I'd remember a man your size.'

'I wasn't there. But I heard about it.'

'And where are your friends?'

'What friends?'

'The ones that were so intent on murdering that Chinese kid.'

'He ain't no kid. He's a miner. They's all small.'

'He's small, all right. So where are the six brave men that decided to work him over?'

'That ain't none o' your business.'

'Fair enough. Then I guess why I'm in town isn't any of your business. Be seein' you around, Luke Wright. It's been nice talking with you.'

It took five or six seconds for Luke to realize he had been dismissed. When it soaked in, he opened his mouth several times to frame an answer, but found no words to do so. Finally he rose to his feet. With a growl that sounded more to Levi like a wounded bear than a man, he grabbed the edge of the table with one huge hand.

'You wanted inta that fight, I'll just let you take the Chink's place,' he growled. He flung the table away from between him and Levi. It landed against another table, from which patrons of the saloon were already moving away when it struck. He lunged at Levi.

Levi came out of his chair swiftly and smoothly, sidestepping the huge man's attack. As the giant of a man crashed into the wall, he clubbed him twice in the kidney's and backed quickly away.

Luke whirled with a wordless roar and charged after him, moving lightly and swiftly. Levi backed into the largest clear area of the floor, just in front of the bar. As Luke charged, he sidestepped again, delivering another crashing blow to the miner's kidney as he lunged past.

Luke grunted with pain and turned back toward his quarry. He hesitated an instant before he lunged after Levi again. Instead of dodging, Levi whirled, extending one leg, delivering a crushing kick to the side of Luke's head with his booted foot.

Luke grunted again, but did not move. Standing in front of him, Levi lifted the other foot and sent three swift, crunching blows to the big man's chin with the heel of his boot.

Luke still did not move. Then he shook his head. He lowered into a crouch and approached Levi more slowly, carefully. In spite of the blows Levi had connected with, Luke was still poised on the balls of his feet, balanced and deadly.

From the crowd that had moved back to encircle the combatants, Levi heard murmured comments.

'Never seen anyone hit Luke that many times afore.'

'Didn't even faze him, either.'

'Wonder what it'd take to knock him down?'

'Ever see Luke fight before?'

'Nope. I seen him kill three men with his fists, but I ain't never seen nothin' I'd call a fight.'

'You see the way that cowboy fights?'

'I seen them slant-eyed heathen fight that way.'

'That's why he took their side. He's one o' them.'

'He don't look like one o' them.'

'Fights like it though.'

'He'll die like it, too.'

'They pay Luke to kill 'im?'

'Doubt it. Just tol' 'im the stranger's a Chink-lover.'

Instead of trying to avoid the miner's charge this time, Levi stepped into it. He delivered a straight right to the bridge of his nose. He put every ounce of strength he had into the punch, then danced away. Blood flew from Luke's nose, but the punch seemed to have no other effect. In spite of Levi's quickness in dancing away, Luke caught him on the ear with a blow that felt like a sledgehammer. Levi's head roared. Flashes of light garbled his vision for an instant.

He ducked back the other way as Luke's fist grazed the other side of his face. He sent a chopping hook into Luke's jawbone and jumped back, making Luke turn to pursue him.

As Luke turned, Levi kicked him twice in the stomach. Luke hesitated just long enough for Levi to catch him with a looping right to the cheekbone. The skin ruptured in a shower of blood. Levi followed it with a sharp hook to Luke's right eye, and blood spurted from it as well.

Luke swiped the blood from his eye and lunged after Levi.

What's it gonna take to knock this guy down? Levi wondered.

Barely evading Luke's charge, Levi hammered his ear with an elbow on the way by, and squared to meet the miner's next charge. He was too slow. As he dodged, Luke's fist connected with his jaw. Even though he was moving away from it, it knocked Levi off balance. His head spun momentarily.

By the time he caught his balance, Luke was on him again.

Gotta slow this guy down, Levi told himself, surprised at the desperation in his own thoughts.

He feinted a left hook, then feinted an overhand right. Then he spun, lashing out with his foot. The heel of his boot caught Luke's kneecap solidly, at a slight angle. Luke winced and tilted to the side. Taking swift advantage, Levi sent two more swift kicks into the kneecap. A groan escaped the huge miner's lips.

Even as the groan broke through, Luke's lips were flattened and spread across his teeth by Levi's fist. Levi squared himself in front of the big man. He began hammering him in the face and head with every ounce of strength and resolve he owned. He lost count of the number of blows he sent into the man's face. Yet Luke stood there as if impervious to them.

Levi's arms felt heavy. Every swing felt like he was forcing his arm through heavy molasses. Every time his fist landed, blood showered out from around it. Still the giant miner stood there.

Levi stepped back, letting his arms fall. Luke's eyes were glazed over. His arms were up, fists clenched, but he did not advance. Levi's breath came in ragged gasps. He shook his head. He gathered himself and leaped into the air. He lashed out with both feet, catching Luke squarely on the chin with one foot and the chest with the other.

41

Levi landed on his back in the blackened sawdust. He rolled over and sprang to his feet as swiftly as he could. Luke still stood there.

Panic surged through Levi. He started to reach for his gun, still strapped into his holster. As he did, the thought flashed through his mind, wondering if even a bullet would stop this guy.

Then Luke moved. He swung at Levi with a looping right that fell short. He followed it with a straight left that went wide. He teetered forward, then gathered momentum. He toppled like a great oak tree, landing in the sawdust with a loud thud.

Levi watched him carefully for a long moment. Luke didn't even make an effort to turn his face out of the sawdust. Levi reached down and grabbed a handful of hair. He lifted the man's head and turned it, dropping it back into the sawdust, but turned to the side so he could breathe without inhaling the sawdust.

He walked back to where he had been seated. He picked up his hat from the floor. He carefully brushed the sawdust from it, using the time to try desperately to calm his ragged breath. When he was sure he could control his voice, he looked around the room.

'Anyone else want to have a go at it?' he asked quietly.

There were no takers. He was thankful for that, at least. He couldn't have swung at anyone hard enough to kill a mosquito, just then.

CHAPTER 5

The air felt crisp and clean. A full moon bathed the earth in an eerie white light. Even the shadows cast by that moon were soft and pale.

'Brighter out here than inside,' Levi muttered to himself.

As soon as he was sure he was out of sight of the Pastime saloon, he stepped into an alley. He swept off his hat. He leaned back against the building. He stood there, sucking in the fresh air, giving his body time to regain a sense of normalcy.

He lifted an arm. Feels plumb quivery, he thought. He's gotta be the hardest man to knock out I ever saw.

After a few minutes he began to feel more normal. He stepped away from the wall. He put his hat back on. He swung his arms back and forth, making them touch in front of him, then behind him. He held out his right hand and studied it in the moonlight.

Swifter than the eye could follow, his hand darted to his holster and lifted, holding a cocked

Colt .45. He nodded in satisfaction. He lowered the hammer and replaced it in the holster. He drew twice more.

He fastened the strap that held the gun in place. He frowned into the night. He unfastened the strap again, tucking it behind the belt, out of the way. He stepped to the head of the alley. Staying in the darkest shadow available, he looked carefully up and down the street. Nothing seemed out of the way.

Still got the knot in my gut, he complained. I thought Luke was probably what the premonition was about. It's still there, though. I hate that feeling!

He took a deep breath. He did two quick deep knee-bends. He flexed his hands, opening and closing his fists. He stepped out into the street.

He started down Front Street, heading for the street that held Ma Corder's boarding-house. Then he noticed a light in the apothecary shop.

Wonder if Sarah's still working, he mused.

He changed directions and walked to the front door of that establishment. The door was locked. He cupped his hand around his eyes and peered through the glass. Sarah was busily arranging things on a shelf. He tapped on the glass.

Sarah jumped and whirled. Her hand flew to her chest, just below her chin.

Jumpy, Levi noted.

Sarah came to the door, speaking through the glass.

'I'm sorry. We're closed.'

'That's good,' Levi replied. 'I didn't want to spend any money anyway.'

'Levi?'

'In the flesh.'

The lock rattled and the door swung open. He stepped in, soaking in the welcoming smile that spread across her face.

'Levi! I didn't expect to see you tonight. I was just catching up on some work I hadn't gotten done, and . . . Oh, Levi! Your face! What happened?'

He grinned. 'Oh, I sorta run into a bear.'

'You look like you tangled with a bear! Here, come sit down. I'll get some water.'

One part of his mind noted that she carefully locked the door behind them. The other part drank in her breathtaking beauty. Obediently he sat down on a chair, turning it backward so he could fold his arms on the top of the chair-back.

Sarah returned with a wash-basin, cloths, a towel, and some jars of something. Carefully she bathed the bruises on his face. She said, 'Your eye is bleeding.'

'It is? I didn't even remember him hitting me on the eye.'

'He hit you just about everywhere,' she insisted. 'Oh, Levi, you're just all battered up. What happened?'

'Do I look that bad? I only remember him hitting me twice. Both of them pertneart knocked me out. Maybe that's why I noticed them.'

'I think it's stopped bleeding,' she said, ignoring

his comments. 'The rest are just bruises. Who did this to you?'

'Fella by the name of Luke Wright.'

She gasped. 'You fought with Luke Wright?'

'Not by choice,' he admitted. 'Hardest man to whip I ever tangled with.'

'I've never heard of anyone being able to stand up to him at all,' she breathed. 'Usually if he decides to fight someone, he just beats them to death. I've never even heard of anyone managing to hit him. How did you get away from him?'

'I didn't. I whipped him.'

She stopped swabbing his wounds and stepped back. 'You what?'

'I whipped him. Left him laying out cold on the floor of the Pastime.'

'You're kidding! Oh, Levi! That's just too, too wonderful! Oh, Levi, I love you for that! He's had this town terrorized for over a year. And you beat him up! Oh, Levi!' She wrapped her arms around him, drawing his face into her bosom, hugging him tightly. In spite of the pain to his battered face, he didn't really mind at all.

She released him abruptly. 'Oh! Oh, I'm sorry! Oh dear, that was terribly brazen of me, wasn't it? I – I don't know why I did that!'

He stood up from the chair and faced her. 'I don't either, but you can do it again any time you want to.'

Her face turned red, but her eyes danced and sparkled. He reached around her shoulders and drew her to himself. She came against him eagerly, turning her face up to him. Her lips were slightly parted, as if in invitation. He couldn't have refused the invitation if he had wanted to. He didn't want to, anyway.

She stepped away, brushing the tips of her fingers across his lips. 'Stop that! You're an injured man. Sit right back down there so I can get something on those bruises.'

'I thought I found something pretty good for them,' he teased. 'At least my lips feel a whole lot better. Now if you'd like to start over here, and just work your way across my face that way, I bet *I'd* feel a whole lot better.'

'Forget it!' She grinned. 'I'd have to fight you off before I got half-way across your face.'

'Would you?'

'Would I what?'

'Would you fight me off?'

She started twice to answer, then closed her mouth. When she did speak her voice was husky. 'Just sit there and let me get you fixed up,' she ordered.

He let it pass, and did as he was told. By the time she'd finished, he had to admit his face felt a great deal better.

'Now let me see your hands,' she demanded.

Docilely he held out his hands, palms up. She took them and turned them over.

'Oh, the salve has made a big improvement! They're not nearly as rough as they were.'

'That's good,' he replied. 'I sure wouldn't want you to think my hands were too rough.'

47

She frowned for an instant, then giggled. She threw his hands down as if disgusted with him.

'You better get out of here, Mr Hill. Go home and go to bed. You're going to be awfully sore by morning.'

He sighed. 'Yeah, I 'spect you're right. I'll tell you what. You give me a kiss that'll tide me over till morning, and I'll leave.'

'I suppose I can manage that,' she offered.

She did.

It was certainly a kiss that was capable of turning a lawman's thoughts away from the dangers that hunted him. It left a song in his head and a silly smile on his lips as he sauntered down the street. It kept him from noticing the furtive movement in the shadows, between two buildings.

Some part of his mind heard the soft click of a rifle hammer coming to full cock. Some hard-bought level of wariness resisted the siren song of love. It remained beneath the lingering smell of Sarah's perfume in his mind. Something sent him diving to the ground, clawing for his gun.

From the darkness between those two buildings, a finger of fire spurted toward him. The explosion of a rifle-shot bounced between the buildings and faded into the night. The angry buzz of a bullet whined past Levi's ear.

He hit the ground and rolled to his feet. He fired two swift shots into the darkness between the buildings. He waited in vain for the tell-tale *thwack* of a bullet striking flesh.

He ran to the side of the street from which the shot had come. The town seemed suddenly, strangely, silent, as if holding its collective breath.

Levi flattened against a store front, and stole a furtive glance into the space between it and the building next door to it. The moonlight was sufficient to assure him nobody was there. He stepped into the opening and sprinted to the back of the building.

Stopping again, he looked around the corner and jerked back. He took an instant to process the image that that quick glance had imprinted on his mind. The shadow of a fleeing man was half a block away, heading toward Bitter Creek.

He flung caution to the winds and ran after the would-be assailant. He was no longer in sight, but Levi fixed his eyes on the place where he had seen him. As he approached the spot, he began to look at the ground. They were far enough from the constant traffic of the street to allow him to look for tracks. He mentally gave thanks for the full moon as he scanned the ground.

Almost at once he spotted the marks of running feet. 'Boots,' he grunted. 'Well, it ain't a miner.'

Following the tracks as swiftly as caution allowed, he moved across relatively open ground. As the tracks led over the lip of a small ravine he slowed. He began to move furtively from one clump of sagebrush to another. His eyes scanned the area before him constantly.

He heard a small sound. He froze in his tracks, listening.

Soft footfalls of a horse approached. He stayed crouched where he was until the horse was nearly to him. Then he stepped abruptly from behind the sagebrush.

'Goin' somewhere?' he asked as he emerged into view.

The horse shied violently. The man swore. His gun, already in his hand, spat fire toward Levi. His horse's frightened prancing made accuracy impossible. The bullet passed harmlessly over Levi's head. He didn't get a second chance. Levi's own gun roared in response. The man grunted and slid off the far side of his saddle. He tried once to get up from the ground, then collapsed.

Levi watched carefully as the horse pranced away, snorting. The man didn't move. Cautiously, Levi approached. He kicked the man's gun away, out of his reach. He hooked a toe under his shoulder and lifted, turning him over. He ignored his already overtaxed muscles' complaints.

The man flopped onto his back. His eyes stared sightlessly at the moon.

'Now I wonder why you were after me,' Levi asked the unhearing gunman.

He sighed and replaced the spent cartridges in his gun. Then he retrieved the dead man's horse. Once again ignoring the complaints of his weary and battered muscles, he hoisted him across the saddle. He used the coiled lariat from the saddle to tie him in place. Then he retraced his steps back into the town, leading the horse

50

with its macabre burden.

At the deputy sheriff's office he tied the horse to the hitch rail. He knocked on the office door. After a few minutes a match flared inside. The yellow glow of a lamp followed. The lock on the door rattled and it opened.

'Sorry to wake a sleeping lawman,' Levi apologized.

'Usually best to leave us and dogs lie, when we're sleeping,' Watkins agreed. 'What you got there?'

'Fella took a shot at me from between a couple buildings. I chased him out to a gully over south. Had his horse tied there. Took another shot at me. He missed. That's all the chances he got.'

Watkins nodded. 'Well, let me get a shirt on. We'll haul aim on up to Ollie's. When we get 'im laid out on a slab, then I can get a good look at him.'

When they had the would-be killer laid onto the table for the undertaker to deal with, the deputy brought a lamp over and held it close to his face.

'Know him?' Levi asked.

Watkins shook his head. 'Nope. Face is familiar, somehow, though. Wonder if maybe I seen it on a flyer.'

'Wanted flyer?'

'Yeah. Get 'em in now an' then. Always take a good look at 'em, just in case I see one of 'em. Never have, though. I see he was ridin' an HH horse.'

'I noticed that. I don't know the brand.'

'Henry Haines,' the deputy informed. 'Has a ranch, oh, twelve, fourteen miles north o' town. Well, let's go back an' have a look at them flyers.'

Back at Watkins's office, the deputy brought a stack of Wanted posters out of a drawer and began to sort through them. Within minutes he said, 'Here he is.'

He handed the poster to Levi. Levi looked at the man's face carefully.

'Sure looks like him, all right. Wiley Anderson. Ollie said he went by the name o' Ward McAllister, didn't he?'

'Uh huh.'

'Wanted in Kansas for murder. Five-hundred dollar reward.'

'That'll be yours, I reckon,' the deputy commented.

Levi shook his head. 'You identified him. You claim the reward. I ain't never took money other than my wages for killing a man. Just as soon not start now.'

'You sure? Five hundred's a lot of money.'

'I'm sure. You can use it.'

'Yeah, I can sure use it. If you don't want it, I'll sure claim it.'

'Fair enough. I might make a ride out to the HH tomorrow, though.'

'What for?'

Levi sighed. 'I'm not sure. Maybe just courtesy. Let the man know I killed one of his hands. Maybe it's just an excuse to get out of town for a day or two.'

Watkins chuckled. 'Mostly the latter, I bet.'
Levi couldn't disagree.

CHAPTER 6

'Take it easy, Buck,' Levi cautioned the eager gelding. 'I know it feels good to get out of town, but
we've got a long ride ahead. Don't use up all your
oats too quick.'

The horse tossed his head in response, and
settled back into the ground-eating trot.

Levi's eyes constantly scouted the country
around him. They noted every movement of bird
or animal, every brush that responded to a
random breeze. He did it without thinking, as a
second nature. It was a habit that had saved his life
many times.

'Not my favorite country,' he confessed to the
always attentive animal he rode. 'Too flat out here,
till it gets up closer to the mountains. Wind'd whip
the barbs off of barbed wire in the winter-time. But
at least the air's clean. No coal-dust underfoot all
the time. No guys blown' black snot on the ground
everywhere you look. I sure don't know how folks
live in a place like that.'

Buck shied ever so slightly as a jackrabbit

exploded from the shelter of a clump of sagebrush and bounded away. Levi chuckled.

'Nervous, are you, fella? You've been cooped up in that livery barn too long.'

At each trickle of water they crossed, he stopped and let the horse drink. About noon he loosened the cinch and removed the bit from the horse's mouth, to allow him to rest and graze for a while. He took some hardtack and jerky from his saddle-bag, slipped the strap of his canteen over his shoulder, hefted his rifle, and climbed to the top of a rocky hill. While he ate his own lunch, he studied the country in a circle as far as his eye could see. The high, dry, clear air made twenty miles look almost like next door. He took note of every gully, the general slope of the land, the location of water, holes and creeks. By the time he finished his lunch he could have drawn an accurate map of a circle extending twenty-five miles in all directions from that hill.

It was approaching supper-time when he trotted through the gate of the HH Land and Cattle Company. Half a dozen dogs barked excitedly. He slowed his horse to a walk, and entered the yard. From the corner of his eye he noticed a cowboy step inside the horse barn and disappear. In less than a minute he caught a glimpse of movement at the haymow door.

'Setting up for trouble, before they even know who I am,' he muttered.

Half a dozen other hands emerged from the cookhouse. They strolled with exaggerated unconcern to widely spaced positions. One leaned against a wall here, another lounged against a corral post there. Their attempt at making the whole thing look casual was almost laughable. They're either a long-rope outfit or been having troubles with someone. he observed to himself.

A big man whom Levi guessed to be in mid forties stepped out onto the long porch that ran around two sides of the main house. At the same time a burly man about ten years his junior walked from the cookhouse to the porch. Instead of climbing the porch steps, the latter arrival took up a position at the end of the porch, standing on the ground.

Smooth, Levi admired. They got me boxed in tighter'n a Christmas top before I even get to the house.

The skin crawled up Levi's back as he reined in before the big man.

'Evening,' he said.

'Evenin',' the big man responded. 'Git down an' come in.'

'Thanks,' Levi said, stepping easily off his horse. 'You'd be Henry Haines?'

The rancher nodded. 'Hank to my friends. You had supper?'

'Well, no. I could use a bit o' grub.'

'I think the boys was just gettin' set to eat a bite. You're more'n welcome to join 'em.'

'I'd be happy to do that. You expectin' trouble, by any chance?'

'Why?'

'Oh, I just noticed the fella in the hayloft when I rode in. Then your boys spread out like they knew just where they were supposed to be, in case I was hostile. You got me boxed in pretty good before I even made it to the house.'

The rancher nodded. 'You got a good eye. You in the habit o' watchin' such things?'

Levi nodded. 'My life sorta depends on it, once in a while. I'm Levi Hill. I work . . .'

'Pinkerton,' the rancher finished.

'You've heard of me.'

'Most folks have. You look some smaller than all the stories have you, though.'

Levi grinned. 'Aw, you don't want to pay much attention to stories. Cowboys gotta have something to tell tall tales about. I 'spect Pecos Bill probably wasn't more'n five feet tall at the time he died.'

Haines grinned back. 'Could be at that. Tall tales sorts get to be the way of a bunkhouse. What brings you here?'

'Oh, just courtesy, I guess. I tangled with a fella iRock Springs yesterday. Fella named Ward Macallister.'

'He's one of my hands. What happened?'

'He took a shot at me from between a couple buildings.'

'That so? Ward didn't miss often. I take it he must've that time.'

Levi nodded. 'He did. I didn't.'

'You killed him?'

'Uh huh.'

Jack Beam, the HH foreman, spoke up from a

corner of the porch. 'You catch mice?'

Haines laughed suddenly, unexpectedly. Levi frowned. Beam's neatly clipped black moustache was quivering.

'What do you mean by that?'

'Story one o' the boys was tellin' yesterday,' Haines explained. 'Fellas accidentally shot a cat that belonged to the boss's wife. He went up to the house, hat in hand, to tell 'er how sorry he was. She asked him if he was gonna replace her cat, an' he allowed as how he'd be happy to do that. So she says, "There's a mouse in the pantry, then. Get busy." '

Levi smiled. 'Well, I don't rightly remember offerin' to take his place, so I ain't sure that fits. I did think I owed it to you to let you know what happened.'

'Why'd he shoot at you?'

'I guess he thought I was there lookin' for him.'

'Why would you be lookin' for him?'

'Well, I didn't know at the time. Watkins looked him up on a wanted flyer he had. His real name's Wiley Anderson. He was wanted for murder in Kansas. Folks tend to talk when I ride into town. I 'spect that when he found out who I was, his conscience convinced him he was the one I was after.'

'You don't say! Well, he was handy with a gun, all right.'

'You didn't know he was on the run?' Levi asked.

Beam stiffened visibly. His hand dropped down beside his gun butt. 'What d'ya mean by that?' he demanded.

'Just asked,' Levi said. 'Did you know he was on the run?'

'You sayin' we're runnin' some kind o' outlaw hideout place here or somethin'?'

Levi did not back down. 'Well, no, I wasn't. But since you brought it up, are you?'

'Why, you . . .' Beam grabbed for his gun.

'Leave it!' Haines barked. 'He's a lawman. He's got a right to ask. Don't be so danged touchy.'

Scowling fiercely at Levi, Beam lowered the gun back into his holster.

'Besides,' Haines continued, 'it ain't a good day for you'n me to get ourselves shot. I seen this man in action once. He'd kill you afore you could cock that thing. Then I'd likely be next, then half the crew afore they could get him. Or didn't you notice the way he's got his horse between him and everyone else 'cept you'n me?'

Beam's eyes darted to Levi's horse, then to the position of every man in the crew. He looked back at his boss, still scowling. Haines turned back to Levi. His tone was conversational, as if he enjoyed the situation and the obvious discomfort of his foreman.

'No, Hill, I sure didn't know Ward was on the run. Or Wiley, you say his name really was. On the other hand, I didn't know he wasn't. You know as well as I do that most outfits don't ask too many questions. Half the boys on the place prob'ly been on the run one time or another. Foolishness, mostly. Fight over a whore, or some dumb thing. Most of 'em turn into pretty good men anyway, if they live long enough.'

'That's a fact,' Levi agreed.

'You got somethin' else on your mind?' Haines demanded.

Levi shook his head. 'Nope. Just thought it'd be neighborly to let you know what happened. Besides, I've been cooped up in Rock Springs for a week and a half. That's a long time for me to be in town. Especially a town as dirty and crowded as that one.'

Haines nodded in agreement. 'Ain't that a fact! I hate that place worse every time I have to go there. I go clear to Green River for supplies when I can, just so I don't have to look at what that danged railroad's doin' to the country with their coal-mines.'

'Maybe the coal'll run out one o' these days, and the land can go back like it was.'

Haines shook his head. 'It never will. Oh, the coal'll run out, all right, Inspect. But after they haul all that stuff up outa the earth an' scatter it all over the ground, the ground won't never go back to bein' fit to graze. It's just ruined. What you workin' on, that keeps you there that long? If you don't mind my askin', that is.'

'It's no secret,' Levi said. 'I'm lookin' into the death of Hiram Dawson.'

'Dawson?' Beam demanded.

'You know him?' Levi responded.

'Of course I knowed him,' Beam said. 'We all did. Him'n Randolph run a good store. Good men. Killed by one o' them Chinese, for treatin' white miners right.'

'Well, that's the story anyway,' Levi agreed.

'So leave it at that,' Beam ordered.

'Why? Am I apt to learn something if I keep digging?'

Beam's anger flashed again. His face turned red. His hand dropped down by the gun butt again, before he thought better of it. He fought to control his temper.

'Some things is best left alone,' he insisted.'

'Why?'

'Sometimes, you dig too deep you end up leamin' things better not known. Some things just shouldn't be talked about. You ain't gonna find out who killed him, anyway. Them Chinese stick together tighter'n a tick to a dog's back. Just drop it an' go on about your business.'

Levi sighed. 'Well, thanks for the advice. I guess I don't have a lot of choice in the matter. When Pinkerton tells me to check it out, I'll check it out.'

When Beam did not respond, he turned back to Haines. 'That invitation to chow down with the boys still good, Hank?'

'Of course! There's empty bunks in the bunkhouse, too. You'd just as well spend the night. Hang around for a day or two if you're a mind to. I might even have a bronc or two for you to top off, if you wanta shake that coal dust outa your hair.'

Levi grinned. 'I just might take you up on that. Probably not tomorrow, though. I ought to ride back and pretend like I'm workin', come mornin'.'

Haines nodded and looked across the yard. 'Leland! Set another plate for supper, will you?'

The cook nodded and waved from the cook3ouse door. He turned and disappeared inside. As he did so, Levi noticed the rifle in his hand. Even the cook! he thought. They're sure expecting trouble from somebody.

He couldn't help wondering if he would find out who before he wanted to.

CHAPTER 7

Anticipation made a tight little knot in the pit of Levi's stomach. Crawling fingers up and down his spine argued heatedly with it.

From a low rise, Levi studied the town of Rock Springs. The sprawling town lay nearest to him. Less than a mile away in the high, clear air, every detail was visible. Beyond the town Bitter Creek meandered lazily along a crooked path of reddish brown earth. Two bridges spanned its gully.

Beyond the creek, the ramshackle jumble of shacks and buildings known locally as Hong Kong sprawled over what had been a sagebrush flat. The sun glinted off tin roofs. Even from a distance it appeared tentative and temporary, as if waiting for the ceaseless Wyoming wind to sweep it away.

The wind that seemed never still did constantly sweep at the black dust. To the right of the town he could see the piles of black slag that marked three different mine entrances. Twin ribbons of shining steel reflected the westering sun, marking the railroad spurs that led to each. The piles of slag squatted like malignant cancers on the earth. They gave the whole town a sense of disease and death that made his skin crawl.

Adding to the sense of malignancy were the boiling racial tensions threatening to erupt. 'Town's just one big boil waiting to bust open,' he muttered to his horse. 'Sure hope I ain't here when all that pus comes rolling out.'

Yet within that troubled tangle of humanity was a bright spot of beauty named Sarah. From their first meeting, they had been drawn to each other as if by destiny. They almost seemed able to see into each other's soul. When he was close to her, Levi's whole being seemed to change. His blood coursed through his veins more quickly. He felt taller. His legs, much too short for his height, seemed to lift him higher. He was keenly aware of the muscles that rippled when he moved.

He was even more aware of everything about her body when she moved. He continually caught himself staring, and had to forcibly tear his eyes from her. At first that seemed to alarm her. As she had grown to know him better, she began to take delight in it. She reveled in her power to distract him, even in mid-sentence, by simple movements of her body. She delighted in his need and excitement when he held her, kissed her. For the sake of propriety, she pretended not to notice his excitement, but she delighted in it nonetheless.

That excitement stored in Levi, even from the distance of the hilltop, as he studied the town. He finally gave up trying to think about anything else and lifted his reins. He let Buck lift quickly to that rapid trot, hurrying him to Sarah.

As he hoped, she was in the store when he arrived. He tied his horse to the hitch rail and walked in. Her face lit up instantly. He felt his blood quicken, even before she spoke.

'Levi! You're back!'

She rushed into his waiting anus. He wished suddenly he had thought to clean his teeth, to chew a sprig of sagebrush or something, in preparation. She didn't seem to mind. Her own breath tasted lightly of cinnamon. Or was it cloves? Did he care? All thoughts except her nearness and his own excitement whirled in circles and were lost in the maelstrom of his rising emotions.

She released him and stepped back abruptly. She cleared her throat. She giggled softly, then smiled. She brushed at the front of her dress. 'Well! I – I think we better find something to talk about, here,' she fluttered.

'I thought we were doing just fine,' he protested.

She giggled again. 'A little too fine, I think,' she corrected. 'We, we're not exactly very private here. Besides, there is such a thing as propriety, you know.'

'There's such a thing as how we feel about each other, too,' he argued.

She brushed at the front of her dress again. 'I know, Levi. I – I want to throw all restraint to the winds as much as you do, but – but, how did your visit to the Haines ranch go?'

Levi sighed deeply. 'Now isn't that just like a woman? Here I am talking about my love, and she wants to know, "How was your trip?" Well, it was lonesome. I missed you.'

'You were only gone two days!'

'That's a long time, when a man's in love.'

'Not even two days,' she amended. 'You just left yesterday morning. Besides, I haven't decided whether you're in love or just in heat.'

'Is there a difference?' He grinned.

She blushed suddenly. 'Stop that! Of course there's a difference.'

'Yeah,' he agreed, 'but they sure do get tangled around each other.'

In a soft, wistful voice, she said, 'I know.' She brightened abruptly. 'Oh, Levi. There have been some people asking about you.'

Alarms sounded in Levi's mind. They pushed the heady surges of his emotions down and away.

'Is that so? People you know?'

She shook her head. 'I've seen one of them. He's a cowboy, but I don't know who he works for. In fact, I'm not really sure he's with any of the outfits around here. There are a couple other guys that are always with him. I think they're mostly just drifters.'

'What do they want with me?'

'I don't have any idea. The one does all the talking. He called you "the Pinkerton", so maybe it has something to do with your job.'

'Another weasel crawling out of the ground,' Levi muttered.

'What?'

'Oh, just mumbling. Everywhere I go, as soon as people find out I work for Pinkerton, all sorts of people seem to surface. It's like one of those water holes that look fairly clean. But if you stir it up, all sorts of scum rises to the top. I seem to have that effect on towns.'

'Do you think that's what he is? Scum, I mean?'

Levi shrugged. 'Hard to tell. Might be somebody with something he's hiding from, so he figures I'm really here looking for him. Or he might be for hire, and somebody that doesn't want me doing my job has paid him to get rid of me. Or, on the other hand, he might be someone that knows something that he thinks will help me.'

'Help you?'

'Sure. When a man gets murdered, you can bet there are people that know what happened, and who did it. Sometimes the knowledge bothers them enough they want to tell about it. A lot of crimes get solved because somebody who knew couldn't handle the guilt of knowing.'

'They wouldn't,' she declared.

'How do you know that?'

She shook her head. 'Oh, I don't mean they wouldn't know anything about Hirarn. I just mean they, uh, they wouldn't be the type that would be likely to feel guilty about anything. They look like the rough sort of men. I think they're here for the trouble.'

His eyebrows shot up. 'Trouble? What trouble?'

'With the Chinese. There's getting to be more

and more talk of getting rid of them. There's no way to get rid of them without just killing them all, or persuading the railroad to stop hiring them. So more and more people are talking about what they're calling a "house cleaning".'

'And you think these men are part of that?'

'Oh, not directly. But there seem to be more and more drifters showing up in town. You know, the kind that follow trouble, hoping they can steal something when trouble starts.'

'I know the type,' he agreed. 'So what do they want with me?'

'I don't know. Maybe they think Pinkerton was hired by the railroad to keep the lid from blowing off the whole thing, so they think that's what you're doing here.'

'Maybe,' he agreed.

'Are you?' she asked abruptly.

'Am I what?'

'Is that what you're really here for?'

'No. I told you. I'm just investigating the murder of Hiram Dawson.'

'That doesn't really make sense. Who would hire Pinkerton to investigate something no more important than one man getting killed? Who did hire you?'

Levi shrugged. 'Not my business to ask, or to tell if I know. I just work for Pinkerton.'

'Then tell them the truth and leave Rock Springs.'

'The truth?'

'Tell them Hiram Dawson was shot by some

Chinese, and the case is closed. Then you can get out of this horrible town.'

'You want me to leave town?'

Her face flared crimson, but she refused to stop what she intended to say. 'Yes. And I would hope that you would ask me to go with you. I don't want you to leave me here. I don't want you to leave me at all. I – I think I love you, Levi Hill. I don't want you to get killed over some stupid murder.'

Her bottom lip and her chin quivered. She clamped her jaw to stop it. He stepped forward and took that chin between his thumb and finger.

'I love you too, Sarah Miles. But I have to do my job.'

He kissed her lightly on the lips. Trying hard to ignore her suddenly overflowing eyes, he turned and walked out the door.

He stopped in his tracks, three steps from the door. On the board sidewalk, three men stood. They had obviously been waiting for him.

'Howdy, Hill,' the one in the center said.

'Evenin',' Levi responded. 'I don't think I know you boys.'

'Is that a fact?' the speaker responded. He spoke to the men on either side of him, without taking his eyes off Levi. 'You boys hear that? He says he don't even know who I am.'

As he spoke, Levi swiftly appraised the situation. The speaker's gun was already drawn, held loosely in his hand, pointing casually at the ground. The other two kept their hands next to their gun butts, but either they had not intended to draw them yet, or he had exited the apothecary store too abruptly to allow them the chance.

The center member of the trio spoke again.

'I 'spect you know me, all right. As a matter o' fact, I got a inklin' I'm the main reason you're here. I'm Klint Scruggs.'

Levi frowned. 'Can't say I've heard the name.'

'Does Texas ring a bell?' Scruggs offered.

'Now I've heard of Texas all right,' Levi agreed. 'You ain't about to tell me you're Texas too, are you?'

One of Scruggs sidekicks laughed. Scruggs shot him a burning glare. The man stifled his laughter, wiping a hand across his mouth. Scruggs turned back to Levi. 'I 'spect you know I'm a wanted man in Texas,' he repeated. 'If you didn't, you do now, so it's all the same. I know who you are, too. That's why I figgered I'd best have my gun in hand a'ready when we settled things.'

As he talked, he raised the barrel of his pistol. He neither knew nor understood what happened next. Levi's hand suddenly had a Colt .45 in it, spouting lead and fire. Scruggs grunted twice in quick succession. He took a step backward and collapsed.

At Levi's first move, both of Scruggs's companions grabbed for their guns. The one on Scruggs's left died before his gun cleared leather. The other followed him across the threshold of death an instant later, just as the tip of his gun barrel moved out of the holster. All four shots from Levi's gun were so closely spaced they sounded almost like a single, long report.

'Every bit as fast as they say.'

Levi whirled, his gun bearing instantly on the speaker. Deputy J.C. Watkins smiled tightly.

'I'd heard you was fast enough to do that,' he said. His voice was steady and even, but his eyes betrayed his fear. 'I only 'bout half-believed it. I'd have given you a hand if you'd waited a bit.'

'Don't guess I had much chance to wait,' Levi said.

As Levi expelled the spent casings from his pistol and replaced them, the deputy continued:

'Fella stopped by an' told me these boys was waitin' here. I figgered you musta come back inta town, an' they was layin' for ya. I was comin' to give you a head's up, an' maybe a hand. Well, Ollie's makin' plenty money off the county since you got here, I'll say that much.'

'You may be too,' Levi countered. 'The one says his name is Klint Scruggs. Says he was wanted in Texas for murder. Might be another reward for you.'

'Well, if you keep it up, I may be able to retire outa this job,' Watkins replied. 'If it's all the same to you, I'd just as soon do it some other way.'

So would I, Levi told himself. So would !.

CHAPTER 8

The knock was brisk, businesslike.

Levi blew out the lamp and laid his book aside. The worn leather binding splayed widely enough for it to stay open at the page he had been reading.

He silently drew his .45. He said, 'Who is it?' then took three swift steps to one side.

'Dr Zastrow. Are you Levi Hill?'

'I am, but I'm not sick.'

A low chuckle followed his words. 'But more than a little cautious, I note.'

Levi stepped across the room silently. He removed the chair that was propped beneath the doorknob. 'Door's open,' he said. 'Come on in.'

The door swung open at once. In the glow of light from the hallway, Levi could see the doctor clearly. He was, perhaps, pushing fifty. He was slightly paunchy. He held a bottle of whiskey and two glasses in his hands. He stepped inside and pushed the door shut with his foot.

'I don't see in the dark too well any more,' the doctor said. His voice was affable, with the hint of a chuckle crouching just behind his words. 'If you'd not mind propping that door shut again and lighting the lamp, I would confess to being much more comfortable.'

'Sorry for the precautions,' Levi offered. 'Been shot at a few too many times.'

'I'm sure that takes a toll on one's disposition,' the doctor agreed.

He stood without moving while Levi replaced the chair beneath the doorknob. Then a match flared, and the wick of the kerosene lamp flamed into life. Levi replaced the chimney of the lamp as he shook the match out.

'What brings you to the refined environment of Ma Corder's Boarding Emporium?' he asked.

The doctor chuckled. 'Ah, yes. Ma Corder. Rock Springs' mother superior and dispenser of sage wisdom and advice. Not to mention the biggest gossip in Wyoming.'

'Gossip's the only pastime most women folk have around here,' Levi countered.

'And they do it well,' the doctor agreed.

'So what can I do for you?' Levi repeated.

The doctor chuckled again. 'The man is all business,' he said, as if to a third party. He held up his two hands. 'I have heard of you, my good man. In fact, I have heard so much of you that I'm sure seventy per cent at least is myth and legend. However, it is said that you are possessed of a rather uncanny knowledge of the classics of literature, that you are roughly competent in both Greek and Latin, and that you are capable of enlightened conversation. A man of education and breeding can develop an overwhelming hunger for that level of companionship in this . . . refined environment, as you put it. I simply stopped by in hopes of finding some good conversation.'

'Who told you that?'

'Well, it has been a matter of several conversations I've been involved in. But before I made a fool of myself, I did bother to chat with Sarah Miles. I have noticed you've developed a very definite attachment there. Anyway, I did visit with her, and she confirmed that you were every bit as well educated and well read as the gossip has indicated. And, I brought some truly fine Irish blended whiskey that I thought perhaps we might share.'

Levi studied the man for a long moment before responding. Seeing nothing except what the man purported to be, he nodded. 'Best offer I've had all day,' he said. 'Have a chair.'

The doctor settled himself into a chair at one side of the reading-table. He sat the two glasses on the table, opened the bottle of whiskey, and poured a modest amount into the bottom of each glass.

'Does your innate sense of caution require you to pick which glass is yours?' he asked.

Levi grinned. 'Naw. Irish whiskey is supposed to kill most anything harmful, isn't it?'

Smiling, the doctor handed him one of the glasses. 'Not necessarily,' he teased. 'In fact, a man of medical training such as myself must know at least half a dozen substances that could be smeared on the inside of a glass which would administer a fatal dose of poisoning, when dissolved in alcohol.'

'Is that so? I've never dealt much with poisons.'

The doctor's eyebrows lifted. 'Really? I would have thought your line of work would require at least a modicum of understanding of poisons and their effects. How to spot signs of poison in a dead body, for example.'

Levi shook his head. 'No, most of the crimes I deal with have the cause of death pretty apparent. When there's a knife sticking out of a man's chest, or half a dozen bullet holes in him, I don't usually have to wonder what killed him.'

'But you have encountered cases of poisoning, haven't you?'

'A few. When I did, though, if I couldn't see what killed the person, I'd talk to the local doctor. Most of them were able to tell me if it was strychnine or something.'

'Ah, yes. Strychnine. The coyote's bane. Effective, but brutal.'

'Most folks who are killing someone aren't too concerned whether it's brutal, so long as it works.'

The doctor chuckled again. 'True, in most cases at least. What are you reading?'

'The *Iliad.*'

'Ah, yes. Fine, fine piece of writing. Have you read . . .'

The conversation rambled over a dozen subjects for an intensely enjoyable two and a half hours. The doctor fished a gold watch out of his vest pocket by the chain. He opened the cover and held it to the lamp.

'Oh, my! Look at the time! I really must go. This has, however, been the most enjoyable evening I have spent for a goodly while. I must say, though, you haven't done my whiskey justice.'

'I don't drink more'n a sip now and then,' Levi explained.

'Never been a drinking man?'

'Never felt I could afford to be. Whiskey slows a man down. A whisker too slow and I'd be a dead man.'

'A wise observation,' the doctor agreed. 'And your present pursuit? How is it progressing?'

'It's not,' Levi admitted. 'I've shaken some scoundrels out of the bushes, but they had nothing to do with Dawson's murder. I'm no closer to solving it than I was a couple weeks ago.'

The doctor's hesitation was obvious. He stared at the floor for a long moment. Then he took a deep breath.

'May I offer some well-meaning advice?'

'I get a lot of that,' Levi lamented. 'I always listen. I don't always take it.'

'That's true with all of us, I assume,' the doctor said. 'Hiram Dawson was . . . a patient of mine. His whole family were my patients. I was, unfortunately, caring for his late wife when she contracted illnesses beyond the scope of my medicine. I continue to care for both Lily and Adelia. Fine girls. They have made a very difficult adjustment, first to the loss of their mother, and now to the loss of their father. I really do not wish to see them upset further. I would very much like to see you accept the findings of the local officer of the law, and leave it at that. Go on to a case with greater importance, Mr Hill. Leave this one as it stands.'

'Is that why you came over here? To talk me into dropping my investigation?'

The doctor cleared his throat. 'I, I must confess to that being part of my motive, yes. I was perfectly honest, however, in my quest for good conversation. And you have not disappointed me! Not in the least! This has been the finest evening of conversation I have enjoyed for many a moon. But, yes, I will candidly admit that much of my reason for being here is to learn whether you are, in fact, a man open to reason. As a reasonable man, I implore you to drop this investigation.'

'Why?

'Well, as I have already said, Lily and Adelia have been through far, far too much already. Even though you have not talked with them directly, aside from that rather cursory questioning the third day you were in town, your investigation is upsetting them a great deal. It has refreshed too many things in their minds better forgotten. Lily was the one who found her father, you know. In their own yard, just outside their back door. Coming in from the shed, where he had just taken care of their milk cow, he was.'

'And they don't want to know who did it?' Levi demanded.

'Oh, they know who did it,' the doctor assured

him. 'At least, they know it was the Chinese, and most of us can't tell one of them from another anyway. And they stick together so tightly that no one of them will ever divulge which individual actually did the shooting. No, they are resigned to just knowing that it was a result of their father's goodness and generosity to the white miners that he died, and they are content with that. I certainly pray that you will be content with that as well.'

'I can't do that.'

'Why not, Levi? There is nothing to be gained by your probing!'

'Maybe. But there's sure a lot of folks doing everything they can to stop me from doing it. If that many people don't want me prodding, there must be a reason.'

'Others have asked you to desist?'

'Yeah, as a matter of fact, they have. Like Watkins. And Haines. And his foreman, Beam, I think his name is. And Sarah. Now you. Next thing I know, the governor'll be stopping by for a chat, so he can ask me to drop it.'

'And would you listen to him.'

'Not if I didn't think I ought to drop it. And I don't. And I won't.'

The doctor sighed heavily. 'Very well. Well, I tried. I do hope you change your mind. And in either case, I hope we can find opportunity to sit and chat again. I am most sincere in saying I have enjoyed the conversation tonight immensely.'

'Me too, till the last five minutes,' Levi countered.

'Then forget the last five minutes,' the doctor said. Then he retracted it. 'No, don't. Think about it. I truly hope you will think about it.'

He removed the chair from beneath the door-knob and let himself out. Levi replaced the chair and sat down, staring at the book he didn't see.

'There's sure something in this deal that folks don't want me finding,' he muttered. 'I wonder if I really want to find out what it is.'

CHAPTER 9

'Are you Sheriff Young?'

He may have been in his mid-hirties. On the other hand, he may have been fifty. His long hair was unkempt. Bushy eyebrows made a solid hedgerow above his eyes, allowing no break at the nose. They were so long they threatened to drop down over his eyes. His long mustache drooped past his lower jaw on either end. The total effect was to make it appear the man was peering through a tangled mass of hair.

The piercing eyes were bright enough to take attention from the facial hair almost at once. They had that same quality Levi had always known his own eyes held. They seemed to look through, rather than at, people. Few men could return a stare from those eyes.

'The last I knew I was, anyway,' the impossibly deep voice rumbled in return. 'What can I do for you?'

'I'm Levi Hill.'

'The Pinkerton guy?'

'The same.'

'Well, well. What interest does Pinkerton have in Green River? It must be almighty important if they sent their best fire-breathin' *deee*tective to deal with it.'

Levi chuckled. 'You mean they sent someone ahead of me to do my job? Where is he? I'll whip 'im!'

Young chuckled in response. 'You do have quite a reputation, you know.'

Levi sighed. 'Yeah, I know. Actually, it helps, sometimes. Mostly it's a pain in the neck.'

'Lower'n that, I'd guess.'

'Can't argue a bit. It seems like people crawl outa the ground trippin' over their guilt as soon as I ride into a place. They mostly just want to kill me, 'cause they're sure I'm after them.'

'Helps clear the air some, though.'

'I s'pose. That wasn't why I took the job, though.'

'Why not?' Young challenged. 'Think about it. You're sent to solve a crime. You solve it. You arrest the villain. Or you kill 'im. Crime solved. One bad guy outa the way. What you've accomplished is get one bad guy outa Wyoming. But in the process, half a dozen other bad guys think you're after them, so they take you on. By the time you're done, there's half a dozen bad guys outa Wyoming. It ain't like you wasn't doin' what you set out to do. Gettin' rid o' bad guys is what it's all about. You just end up doin' a sight more'n you set out to. I can't see how that's a bad thing.'

'Maybe. But then, you aren't the one getting shot at in the process.'

Young laughed shortly. 'That makes it even better, from my side o' the fence. Better you than me.'

'You're all heart.'

'That's my nature. What can I do for you?' he repeated.

'You've heard of Hiram Dawson?'

'Of course. But that's over at Rock Springs. Not here.'

'That's where I've been for the past three weeks.'

'You've met Watkins, then?'

'Several times. Talked with him my first day in town. He seems less than interested in having the murder investigated.'

'That so? Not interested, or just figures it's a waste of time?'

'I'm not sure. I just thought I'd ride over and visit with you about it. Maybe you'd have a different slant.'

'I doubt it. There ain't much doubt it was one or another of the Chinese. They pretty much act together, so the chances of finding out which individual did it are somewhere between slim and none.'

'You're sure it was the Chinese?'

Young hesitated a long while. He pulled one end of his mustache as he pondered. At last he said, 'Well, I'm sure you've sized up the situation over there. The Union Pacific has shipped in hundreds of Chinese to work the coal-mines. That puts that many white men out of jobs, though why any white man would want that job is beyond me. But they do. Now they ain't got 'em. To add fuel to that fire, the UP sells the Chinese all their tools an' supplies at less than half the price they'll sell 'em to white men for. That makes the white men hate the Chinese even more. Then there's the natural antagonism any race feels for someone that don't speak their language, don't look and act like them, an' so forth. Then Dawsons start sellin' tools an' supplies to the whites for even less than the UP sells 'em to the Chinese for. Now the Chinese are gettin' mad at the whites right back. Nothin' like bein' hated to teach a man to hate. By this time, both bunches over there hate each other so much I don't hold much hope of it ever workin' itself out.'

'Then what will happen?'

'War.'

'War?'

'More like a massacre, likely. Sooner or later, one side or the other's gonna start killin' folks. When it does, and I 'spect it already did with Dawson, then the other side's got to kill someone to get even. Then the other side has to kill someone to get even with the other side for gettin' even with them. The only thing that's keepin' it from happenin' right now, I'm thinkin', is that nobody's proved it was the Chinese that killed Dawson. Now if you come in there an' do your investigatin' for Pinkerton, you may prove that. From the sake o' doin' your job, that'd be a good thing, I 'spect. But from the sake o' the town, that'd be a disaster. If you prove the Chinese killed Dawson, then somebody's gotta kill a Chinese, just to get even. Then the party's opened up, and there won't be no way in hell to stop it.

Levi pondered the words in silence for a long time before answering. After a time he said, 'So you think Watkins and the others and there have been quite a few others – who tried to get me to stop looking into it, are trying to keep that from happening?'

'That'd be my guess. If I could, I'd sure add my voice to the chorus an' sing the same song.'

'If you could.'

'If I could. I don't guess I can, very well. I take my job seriously too. I can't be an officer of the law and ask somebody not to investigate a murder. But I can tell you, just between you an' me, that I stayed plumb outa that one. I let J.C. do it his way. I didn't interfere. I didn't ask him to poke into it any deeper. He's my deputy, an' I trust his instincts. If he says it oughta stop right where it is, I sure ain't gonna argue with him.'

'What if I were to prove it wasn't Chinese that killed him?'

The facial hair through which the sheriff peered bobbed and bounced as if by its own volition.

'You got some reason to think it wasn't?'

'I just asked.'

The hairy brush through which the sheriff eyed him rustled and swayed. 'Then you might open a whole different can o' worms. I wouldn't be half as scared o' that can o' worms as I am o' you bein' able to prove it was a Chinese. If it was somebody else, there'd be a different sort o' reason, an' it wouldn't likely blow the lid off the town. Watkins could handle that. Trouble is, how you gonna know, till you find out?'

'Good question. How am I?'

'You ain't. So you're gonna take a chance on blowin' Rock Springs wide open, just to see if you can keep from doin' it. Who wants to know so bad, anyway?'

'Pinkerton don't always even tell me who hires 'em.'

'Yeah, but they did this time.'

'How do you know that?'

' 'Cause you didn't just up an' tell me you don't know. You gave me that run-around sorta answer. That means you won't lie, but you want me to think you don't know. Which means you know.'

Levi smiled. 'Being an honest man has its draw-backs,' he admitted.

'And its rewards. Especially in this country. So who hired Pinkerton?'

'Dawson's family. His folks.'

'What's their interest?'

'Something about the girls. They stand to inherit a substantial amount from their family. They want to be sure the girls, or Hiram's brother, weren't involved in the murder.'

The clumps of facial brush bobbed and swayed violently for half a minute.

'Why in thunder would they be involved?'

'I don't have any idea,' Levi admitted. 'I've talked with both of the girls. They seem like they're good girls, but they've been through a lot. They're pretty bashful. Wouldn't hardly talk to me. Kept their eyes on the ground, mostly. But they didn't seem to be hiding anything.'

'You didn't push 'em any?'

'Didn't have any reason to. I'd have to have a pretty good reason to push a couple teenage girls, I guess. Anyway, they're just kids. I don't see any way they could be involved at all. It ain't like they had anything to gain from his death. They just lost the only parent they had left, that's all.'

Young nodded his head. 'But they want some sorta proof it was the Chinese. Or at least that the girls didn't have any connection to it.'

'That's the way I've got it sized up.'

'So if you do your job, you'll blow the lid off of Rock Springs. If you don't, a couple o' well-deservin' girls will lose a whoppin' big inheritance. That's betwixt a rock an' a hard place, if you ask me.'

'Try asking me. I'm the one in it.'

'Like I said, with folks crawlin' outa their holes to shoot at you, better you than me.'

'Like i said, you're all heart.'

'I try to be sympathetic.'

'By the way, I'd appreciate it if nobody knew who's behind the investigation, or why.'

'You didn't tell Watkins?'

'I haven't told anybody, except you.'

89

'OK. I appreciate the confidence. I'll keep it that way. What're you gonna do?'

'Do my job, I guess. As long as I'm taking Pinkerton's money, I don't have much choice.'

'Well, I'd wish you luck. I just don't know what that'd mean.'

'I guess that'd mean I find some cowboy that gets drunk and tells me he mistook Dawson for his old foreman and shot him when he was too drunk to see straight. That'd let everybody off the hook.'

'That's real likely to happen.'

'I didn't say it was likely. I just said that'd be lucky.'

'Well, if you find out it was Chinese, give me a few days to get the army in there before you go announcin' it to the town.'

'You think it's that serious.'

'It could get that serious over there, real quick.'

Levi knew it wasn't empty talk. Just then he wanted more than anything in the world to just be someplace else, with a different assignment. Like maybe fight the Sioux nation single handed.

CHAPTER 10

Tension stalked the streets of Rock Springs. People who hurried from store to store cast nervous glances in all directions as they walked. Here and there small clusters of people talked. The quick movements of hands and arms, the jabbing of fingers at one another, the bobbing of heads in cadence, bore testimony to agitated conversations.

Skin crawled up Levi's back. 'I never saw a town so primed for trouble,' he muttered.

Even his horse agreed, blowing nervously in reply. He thought about stabling Buck in the livery barn, then going to see Sarah. Then he decided he'd stop and see Sarah first. Then he decided he'd do both. He'd stop and say 'Hi' to Sarah, then go stable his horse and clean up, then come back to spend the evening with Sarah. The thought of that quickened his blood. He sat a little straighter in the saddle. He nudged the horse to a swifter walk.

He tied up the horse at the hitch rail in front of the apothecary shop. In his mind he was already experiencing the feel of Sarah's body pressing against his, the smell of her hair, the excited squeal of welcome as she saw him, the taste of her lips.

He stepped in the front door of the store. The scene that had been replaying in his mind played itself out exactly as he had pictured it. Nothing was left out. Nothing held any disappointment.

When the moment of excitement passed, she stepped back. He anticipated, a split second ahead of the action, the way she would brush at the front of her dress, then brush back the unruly strands of hair from her face. Her eyes danced and sparkled.

'Back from Green River already? I was afraid you might stay another day.

'What, and give some lover-starved cowboy a chance to spot my girl? Not a chance!'

He was rewarded with a quick giggle. 'If you were that worried, why did you leave at all?'

'Duty, milady. Duty.'

'You smell a little dutifiil too,' she teased.

'I didn't know duty smelled like sweat,' he grinned.

'I didn't either, till you told me what the smell was,' she shot back. 'Why don't you go get some of the duty scrubbed off, then you can come back here and I'll cook you some supper.'

'Best offer I've had all day,' he responded. 'Is your dad here?'

'No, why?'

'Oh, just had a couple questions I was going to ask him. I'll ask him at supper.'

'He won't be there.'

Levi's eyebrows shot up. 'Oh? Where's he?'

'He and mother went to Laramie.'

'Laramie! Business?'

Sarah hesitated a moment before answering. 'They want to talk to the governor. They want him to send some troops here. They think a military presence might settle the talk down. It's getting pretty scary, listening to the things people are saying.'

He nodded. 'It is that, for a fact. So you're going to cook supper just for me and you?'

'Sure! Isn't that all right?'

'Sounds good to me,' he understated.

It was far too much to ask that a man could keep his mind on impending danger and Sarah at the same time. That's why it took him an instant longer than it normally would have to spot the pair standing in the street. When he did, he stopped in his tracks. He heard Sarah's quick intake of breath inside the front door of the store.

He stepped quickly to one side to move Sarah out of any line of fire. It was instantly obvious to his seasoned eye that the pair were hired gunmen. Who had hired them didn't really matter at that point.

'Howdy, Hill,' one of them said. His voice was as cool and casual as if over a cup of coffee.

'Evenin' boys,' Levi responded, trying to sound just as casual. 'Do I know you?'

'hope,' the speaker responded. 'Just here to do a job.'

'For who?'

93

'Doesn't matter.'

'Might, to me.'

'Not likely. I've heard you're good. So'm I. So's Wes. We don't neither one think you're good enough to beat either one of us. But just to be on the safe side, we thought we'd be sure, 'cause there ain't no way you're good enough to beat us both.'

'Which one prefers to be the one to die, just in case I don't get you both?'

'Don't matter none. Any time you wanta open the show, go for your gun.'

The door of the apothecary store suddenly slammed shut with such force the front of the building quivered. Instantly Levi stepped to the side, moving behind a post that supported the porch roof. As he did, his gun was already out, bucking in his hand.

Both of the gunmen were fast. Really fast. Their guns were in their hands at almost the same instant as Levi's was in his. Only the distraction of the slamming door gave Levi an ever-so-slight edge. Slivers flew from the porch post as Levi's gun blazed. His shots and those from both gunmen blended together into a staccato roar that ended as quickly as it had begun.

One of the gunmen flopped on to his back. The other simply wilted on to the ground. The door of the apothecary store flew open. Sarah rushed out, eyes darting up and down Levi. She gasped at the blood running down his arm.

'Levi! You're hurt!'

He shook his head. 'Just tore up some by those

wood slivers, I think,' he said. 'Boy, those two were fast. Either that or I'm slowin' down. They'd've had me if you hadn't slammed that door.'

'You mean I really did save your life?'

'That's exactly what I mean,' he affirmed. 'That was pretty cool thinking.'

'Couple more snakes crawl outa the ground?'

Levi turned to face the voice of J.C. Watkins.

'Not this time,' he disagreed. 'These boys were hired just to get rid of me.'

'You don't say! They told you that?'

'One of 'em did. Said they were just doing a job. I asked who hired 'em, but he didn't say.'

Watkin's lips compressed to a thin line. 'Well! That puts a different spin on the whole thing, don't it. Now who'd wanta stop your investigatin' bad enough to hire a couple killers?'

'Or knew where to find 'em and hire 'em,' Levi added.

'Oh, Levi,' Sarah implored, 'come in and let me get that arm fixed.'

'You get hit?' Watkins asked.

Levi shook his head. 'Just slivers off the post. Their aim was a whisker off.'

Watkins took a deep breath. 'Well, I'll have Ollie take care o' your leavin's, then I'll riffle through the posters again. I ain't likin' this, though.'

'Me neither,' Levi agreed. 'Less all the time.'

Sarah cleaned his wounds and removed the slivers that had penetrated his arm. By the time she finished, the bleeding had stopped, and he left. An hour and a half later he was back.

'Wow! You look a lot better,' she praised.

'Smell better too,' he promised. 'Care to get close enough to check it out?'

She did. 'You even chewed on a clove, didn't you?' she teased. 'What, do you think I'm just waiting for you to walk in here and kiss me just anytime?'

'Aren't you?'

'Not right now,' she argued. 'I'm busy closing up this store so we can go home and I can fix you some supper.'

Even the constant threat of attack, of race riots, of insoluble crimes seemed to retreat to some far away part of the globe as he walked her to her house. He was surprisingly aware of the emptiness of the house, its silence reminding him constantly that he and Sarah were there alone.

After the finest supper he could remember, he helped her wash the dishes. They talked for a long while. Conversation kept coming back to the reason he was there.

'Lily really wants you to just drop it, you know,' she said for the umpteenth time.

'I still don't understand why,' he argued.

'She asked me what our intentions were,' Sarah injected.

'Our intentions?'

'You and me,' Sarah clarified. 'She wanted to know if . . . that is . . . if you had said anything, I mean, about when your job here is finished. Going away.'

He brushed a strand of hair back from her

cheek, feeling overwhelmed as always by her beauty.

'I guess I haven't thought an awful lot about that,' he admitted. 'I haven't wanted to think past just ... well ... I don't know. It's not smart for someone with a job like mine to go falling in love with someone. It's just not in the cards.'

'But it could be.'

'How? I'm never in one place more than a few months at most. They send me all over the territory. It sure wouldn't be any life for a woman.'

'It would for me, if I were with you.'

'Yeah, but what about when kids come along. That sorta seems to happen, you know.'

She was silent for a while. 'I don't know. I hadn't thought that far ahead. But there are other jobs than Pinkerton. You could have any sheriff's job in Wyoming, just by running for it. Then we could live in one place, and you could still be a lawman.'

'I don't know. I've never really thought about being that kind of lawman. Anyway, it's getting late. I'd best be getting back to Ma Corder's, and get some sleep.'

As he stood, she rose and came into his arms. He kissed her, surprised by the fire he felt in her, and by the responding fire he felt building in him.

'Levi, you don't have to go,' she said softly.

'What do you mean?'

'You can stay, if you want to. We have the house to ourselves. I know you love me as much as I love you. I know you're not the type to just take advantage of someone and then ride off into the sunset or something. I don't have to wait any longer for us to – to physically seal our love. And I'll go anywhere in the world with you, be whatever you want me to be. That has to be more important to you than keeping up this investigation any longer, doesn't it?'

Levi fought against the rush of blood throbbing in his temples. His body screamed in response to her closeness, her willingness. He tried to swallow. The lump in his throat made it almost impossible.

He forced himself to take a deep breath. He pushed her away from him, just enough to let him think. Every fiber of his being stretched toward her, yearning to pull her back against him, to envelop her into himself, to sate his surging desires. At the same time, the alarm bells clanging in the back of his mind kept getting louder.

'You mean I can have you, if I just agree to drop the investigation?' he asked.

'Oh, Levi! Darling! Don't make it sound like that! We do love each other! Don't we? I've never loved anyone like I love you. I want to belong to you. Completely. Now. Tonight.'

'You didn't answer my question. Did Lily ask you to do this?'

An instant's hesitation gave him the answer she denied. 'Why, Levi! Of course not! Oh, you know we talk all the time. Lily and Adelia are my best friends in the world. They know how much I love you, that you love me. That's no secret.'

'But if I have you, that means I have to drop the investigation,' he pressured.

'Stop making it sound like that! I just don't want the man I love, the man I belong to, the man I'm inviting into my bed, to cause my best friends so much pain and anxiety. I love you, darling. With all my heart.'

'I don't like deals that come with strings attached,' Levi snapped. 'And I sure don't like some woman trying to use her body to buy me off from doing my job. Tell your friends it didn't work. Levi didn't take the bait.'

'Levi! No! Don't leave!'

He could hear her sobbing softly as he closed the door on his way out.

CHAPTER 11

It started at Mine No 6. Early the morning of 2 Septembe. things began to boil over. Isaiah Whitehouse and William Jenkins clashed with the Chinese who were working a room in the mine. That room had been given to Whitehouse and Jenkins the day before.

'Hey,' Whitehouse called. 'You guys get outa here. This here's my room to work.'

'Pit boss ally swine give us room,' one of the Chinese replied.

'Like a pig's ear he did,' Whitehouse responded. 'Git outa here or I'll ram this pick right where it'll do the most good.'

The Chinese miner swore furiously, calling Whitehouse several names in flawless English. He swung his pick at Whitehouse's head.

Isaiah ducked under the blow and let loose a straight right that connected solidly with the Chinese miner's chin. He dropped his pick and landed on his back. At once he began screaming and yelling in Chinese.

Other Chinese began to appear as if by magic, brandishing picks, shovels and tapping needles. Other white miners responded, bursting into the room at top speed. Instantly picks, shovels, and anything that could be used as a weapon began swinging. Whitehouse was caught squarely in the stomach with a pick. He doubled up and crumpled to the floor. Instantly three white miners circled him, fighting back.

'Hey! Break it up in here!' a foreman yelled, wading into the fray. Behind him half a dozen other foremen spread into the mêlée, separating combatants, yelling for order.

Five Chinese were lying still, in pools of blood. Three white miners sat against a wall of coal, nursing wounds.

'You Chinee boys,' the foreman yelled, 'get your wounded and go topside. No work today. Go home.'

Reluctantly the two sides separated. Glaring menacingly at each other, each side clustered together. The Chinese helped three of their wounded to their feet, and picked up the other two. In a matter of minutes there were only white miners left.

'You boys stay right here for twenty minutes,' the foreman ordered. 'The rest of the foremen are escorting the Chinese out. When they're gone, you boys can leave too. There ain't gonna be no more work today. We're shuttin' 'er down till you boys cool off.'

Without another word he turned and strode from the room.

The twenty minutes were almost up when Jim Evans, superintendent of Mine No 6, appeared at the entrance to that room. He was met with an immediate outpouring of complaints, threats, and anger. He tried twice to quiet the miners so he could speak. They were in no mood to listen. Escorted by four of his foremen, he beat a hasty retreat.

The white miners surged out of the entrance in a roiling mass.

'Come on boys,' one of them called to the others, 'we may as well finish it now, as long as we commenced.'

The rest shouted agreement. In a body they started toward town, with the unspoken consent of meeting at the Pastime saloon.

Like magic the word spread. White miners from all the other mines learned what was happening as if it were carried through the veins of coal into the rooms they worked. In small groups they walked out of their mines as well. Within an hour the Pastime was overflowing. Front Street was filled with miners. Steady streams of them went in and out of the saloon refilling their glasses and mugs. Talk of vengeance against the Chinese grew into a steady, ominous rumble in the street.

Levi strode through the door of J.C. Watkins's office.

'Looks like big trouble,' he said without preamble.

'Don't I know it!' Watkins agreed. 'I been tellin' Young fer weeks we hadta get the army here, or things'd boil over.'

'Miles went to Laramie to get the governor to send gem a few days ago.'

'Yeah. He had the same luck I did.'

'None, huh?'

'None. Governor says he can't call 'em in. Says Washington has to do that. He ain't got the authority. He sent a wire, but they wired back that if there ain't no real trouble yet, they can't send 'em in.'

'It's too late now, anyway,' Levi observed. 'I've never seen a mob gettin' that mad that quick.'

'Me either,' Watkins agreed. 'I don't mind tellin' ya, I'm scared enough to wet my pants. I got no idea how to stop it.'

'You might be able to get enough businessmen together to make a show of force. Force 'em to break it up an' go home.'

Watkins swore. 'Half the businessmen are in the mob! Women, too. I seen two women out there with shotguns, eggin' everybody on.'

'You're kidding!'

'I kid you not!'

'Maybe I could get over to Green River. Maybe Young could get a bunch to come over from there. Even fifteen or twenty men would make a big enough group so a mob wouldn't be apt to challenge 'em.'

'I wouldn't bet on that. Right now, I think this bunch'd take on the United States Army.'

'So what are you going to do?'

'Well, I'm gonna go over an' tell both the Pastime an' the Pioneer they gotta close up shop. If we stop the flow o' whiskey, maybe the mood'll start to change. If we can keep anyone from doin' anything to start a riot till they sober up some, we may have a chance.'

'I still think Young's the best bet.'

'Well, you ride hell fer leather over there an' git 'im, then. But tell 'im not to show up here with less than twenty good men. Any less than that'd be worse than nothin'. If you ride hard, you can be back by sundown. That's when it's most likely gonna boil over.'

'Buck can run that far, if he has to,' Levi promised. 'I'll have to get a different horse to ride back.'

'Then get to it.'

Levi half-ran to the livery barn, saddled his horse, and headed out of town. Too late to dodge, he saw him. From behind a clump of sage-brush beside the road, a man stepped with a rifle trained squarely on Levi. Fire flashed from the tip of the barrel. Levi braced for the impact of the slug.

An angry whine passed by his ear. As if in slow motion, he watched the gunman topple over. He hauled on Buck's reins, skidded him to a stop, dived from the saddle.

He rolled to his feet, gun in hand. The gunman lay where he had fallen. A grinning Chinese miner stood beside him. A tapping needle hung in his hand. Recognition flooded through Levi.

'Tang Lu! Boy, you're a sight for sore eyes. That guy had me dead to rights.'

'He think kill you,' Tang agreed.

'What are you doing out here?'

'Tlying to see what go on in town. Vely big tlouble, I think. See fella watch you. Come hele, hide in blush. I think he tly kill you. I sneak alound, sneak up behind. Almost too slow.'

'Well, you weren't. I'm much obliged. You saved my life.'

'Ally same both way now,' Tang grinned. 'You save Tang, Tang save you. Ally same both way.'

'Yeah, we're even all right. Listen, Tang, you better head home and tell your people they best get outa Hong Kong. Tell 'em they'd best just pull out an' hide out in the rocks an' sagebrush south o' town. All hell's going to bust loose in town, I'm afraid. If somebody starts it, they'll come looking for any Chinese they can find. Any they find are likely to die. If they have to leave everything, tell Pem to do it. Just get out of town. I'm on my way to Green River to get the sheriff, and some men to help. Until I get back, you get your family and all your people outa town.'

Tang nodded repeatedly. 'I tell. I listen. Ally same bad things happen, I think. Not think most leave, though. They stay to fight if have to.'

'Listen, Tang, they can't fight this. Not many of your people have guns. All the people that'll be coming after you do. There's no way you can stand against guns with picks and shovels.'

'I telly. I tly. No plomise.'

'OK. Do what you can do. And thanks.'

'Ally same both way.'

Levi whirled his horse and jammed the spurs to his side. Buck leaped forward, hitting full stride in three jumps. He ran easily, smoothly. Levi leaned forward across the saddle horn to reduce the wind drag as much as possible.

For two hours the great gelding ran full out. In that two hours Levi covered the entire distance of twelve miles from Rock Springs to Green River. When Green River came into sight, he slowed the horse to a swift trot.

The lathered horse attracted so much attention that traffic on the sidewalks had stopped when Levi stepped off his horse in front of the sheriffs office. As he did, Sheriff Joe Young stepped out to meet him.

'Afternoon, Hill. Tryin' to kill your horse?'

'Sure hope not,' Levi said. 'He's been run hard before. He's got a lot of bottom.'

'He must. What's goin' on?'

'All hell's about to bust loose over at Rock Springs. Watkins sent me to ask for some help. He wants you to come with at least twenty good men.'

'What's goin' on?'

'There was some kind of a fight in one of the mines this morning. Turned into a brawl between the whites and the Chinese. All the mines shut down. Everybody started drinking and telling each other how much they hate the Chinese. They're talking of going over to Hong Kong and wiping it off the map.'

'Are they serious?'

'They're serious. I've never seen a mob in that bad a mood. I've seen some mobs get out of hand a few times. I've never seen anything that scared me like this deal does.'

'So you agree with J.C?'

'You bet! The only thing I don't agree with is, I'm not sure we can get a bunch of men back there in time to stop it.'

'Hey, Sheriff!' a man in the street called. 'Look!'

He was pointing to the east, standing in the middle of the street. Young and Levi walked together to the center of the street. Low on the eastern horizon a dark smudge appeared to be spreading.

'That's smoke!' the man who had called out said. 'You think it's a prairie fire?'

As they watched the smudge of smoke grew and began to ascend into the sky. Levi felt as if he had been kicked in the stomach.

'That's coming from Rock Springs,' he said.

'Have to be an awfiil big fire to see the smoke twelve miles away,' Young observed.

'Hong Kong.'

'Chinatown?'

Levi nodded. 'Looks like it's started. Looks like they're putting the whole town to the torch.'

'God help us!'

'God help the Chinese,' Levi corrected. 'The mood that mob was in, I'm guessing they shot every Chinese they could find. I sure hope they listened to Tang.'

'Who's Tang?'

'Tang Lu. The Chinese kid I kept 'em from killing when I first rode into town. I sent him to tell everyone in Hong Kong to get out of town. I told'em to just run like rabbits out into the sage-brush and rocks and hide out till things settled down. I sure hope they listened to 'im.'

Watching the growing spire of smoke, Young replied, 'There's a whole lot o' dead Chinese over there if they didn't.'

He had no idea how right he was.

CHAPTER 12

Hoofbeats thundered into town. A lathered horse was hauled to a stop in front of the office of Sheriff Joseph Young. J.C. Watkins spilled from the saddle and burst through the door of the office.

'Sheriff! You gotta come!'

'What's happenin', J.C?'

'It's . . . it's . . it's awfiil! All hell's busted loose. I ain't never seen nothin' like it in my life. If you'da asked me, I'da told ya that human beings won't never actually act like that. I'm tellin' ya, Sheriff, you gotta get there, or there ain't gonna be no Chinese left by mornin'.'

'Simmer down and tell me what happened, J.C.'

Levi watched and listened in silence as J.C. Watkins spilled his tale.

'It started with a fight at the mine. The feelin's twixt the Chinese an' the whites been gettin' bad lately. Real bad. An' the UP just keeps makin' 'em worse. Anyway, there was a fight, an' several fellas got hurt purty bad. They pertneart kilt Isaiah Whitehouse. I don't know. He may die yet. Hit 'im

111

in the gut with a pick. I think he's all busted up inside.'

'So get on with what happened.'

'Well, the mines all closed up, 'cause all the miners quit workin'. The whites, 'cause they was gettin' all het up, an' the Chinese, 'cause they was startin' to get scared. So the mines all closed up. That sure didn't help none! Then all the miners started congregatin' down town, an' drinkin' like there wasn't gonna be no likker tomorrow. Along about noon, me'n Levi, there, decided we oughta shut down the saloons. They wasn't none too happy about it. They was doin' land-office business, I'll tell ya.'

'But they did shut down.'

'Yeah. Far's I know they did. I didn't see any of 'em servin' any more, anyway. But it was too late. They started collectin' into mobs in the street. Then it was like somethin' just come in an' took over. I don't know how to say it. It seemed like somethin' evil just come in an swept along the street like evil wind er somethin'. People started talkin' crazy. Talkin' about how they oughta get rid o' the Chinese once an' for all. Kill 'em all. Burn 'em out. String 'em up to anything they could hang 'em on. Cut 'em to pieces.'

'Mob fever.'

'It was somethin', all right. Women, too. Women from the businesses, or what had husbands in business, was out in the street eggin' everybody on.'

'Women? You don't say!'

'Then a couple Chinese guys come by, headin' for one o' the bridges. They was hurryin', like they knowed the lid was about to blow off. An' somebody just up an' shot one of 'em.'

'Did you see who?'

'No. It was just a shot rang out from one o' them mobs o' fellas. An' the Chinese guy goes down, and it . . . it . . . aw, Joe, I ain't never seen nothin' like it. Everybody in the street started che~erin', like some really great thing just happened. The other Chinese was tryin' to get the one what was shot up, to help 'im acrost the bridge, and somebody shot him too. Then everybody cheered again.'

'That's all it'd take, I 'spect.'

'It sure was! People started hollerin' "Let's go get the rest o' them rat-eatin' pagans", an' it was like openin' a gate to a corral fiill o' wild cattle. They just plumb stampeded over acrost the bridges, an' started shootin' every Chinese they could see. It didn't matter whether it was a man or a woman. It didn't matter whether they was runnin' away er standin' still. They was just shootin', like they was tryin' to get rid o' rats.'

Levi spoke for the first time. 'Were all the Chinese still there?'

Watkins shook his head. 'I don't think so. There was a lot, but not near enough for the mines bein' closed down an' all. A whole bunch of 'em musta figgered out what was comet', an' got out. But there was a whole lot what didn't.'

'We saw the smoke.'

'Yeah. They started goin' through their shacks to haul out anyone hidin'. Then someone hollered "Why do that? Burn 'em out. We're gonna burn this eyesore off the face o' the earth anyhow, so let's roast a few o' them disciples o' Confucius." Then they started torchin' every building they came to.'

'With people inside?'

Watkins nodded. 'Some of 'em. People'd come runnin' out, on fire, an' they'd shoot 'em. Or just laugh an' watch 'em burn to death. You could hear some of 'em inside screamin'' while they burned. It was awful. An' there wasn't one thing I could do about it. I yelled and hollered at 'em. I even threatened to shoot some of 'em. They just laughed at me an' run over me. I couldn't fight the whole town. You gotta get a posse together an' get over there.'

Young shook his head. 'Me'n Levi been tryin'. We can't get one man to ride with us.'

'Well, wire for the army!'

'I been doin' that. I wired Governor Warren. He said he couldn't do nothin', 'cause they're federal troops an' we're a territory, not a state. So I wired the army. General Howard said they had to have an order from the president. So I wired President Cleveland. Somebody in his office wired back that he's on vacation, an' can't be reached.'

Watkins stared in disbelief. 'So what are they goin' to do?'

Young sighed heavily. 'Well, they're workin' on it. They're tryin' to get ahold o' the president, so he can give the word. The army's gettin' all geared up to come, just as soon as they get their orders. But it'll be two er three days at best.'

'So what do we do in the meantime?'

'We'll ride over there,' Young affirmed. 'We'll try to do what we can. I honestly don't know what that'll be, but we got to try.'

'We?'

'You'n me an' Levi.'

'Three of us, against the whole town?'

'There's gotta be a few level heads in town.'

'If there were, they was hidin' real good!'

'I 'spect they were. If they had any sense, they were. They wouldn'ta done nothin' against a mob 'cept get themselves killed if they tried. Go over to the hotel. Get some sleep. We'll be in the saddle headin' out by sun-up.'

'You gonna wait till mornin' to even go?'

Young looked at his deputy for a long while. 'Do you want to ride into there in the dark?'

Watkins swallowed twice. He took off his hat and slapped the dust from it.

'Prob'ly not,' he conceded.

True to his word, Young, Watkins and Levi were in the saddle, trotting swiftly from Green River as the sun peeked over the eastern ridges. As if it saw the carnage at Rock Springs, the sun immediately took refiige and hid behind a cloud. It did not show its face for the rest of the day.

Rock Springs was a scene from a nightmare. Groups and clusters of drunken men reeled through the streets, shooting into the air, recounting tales of the previous day's butchery, laughing uproariously. Windows of businesses were boarded up. Only the saloons seemed to be operating, and they were doing business at such a rate Levi wondered how long it would take their stocks to run dry.

The mobs in the street completely ignored them. Nobody challenged them. Nobody apologized. Nobody seemed afraid or showed either sorrow or compassion. They seemed oblivious to everything except their own venting of all the pent-up frustrations and anger of the previous months.

'I need to stop here,' Levi announced.

'I thought you an' her was busted up,' Watkins said.

'We are, I guess. But I still care about her. I want to know she's all right.'

'Her dad is one I thought we could count on,' Watkins replied.

'I'm sure you can,' Levi agreed. 'He's even been to see the governor to try to get troops in here before this all happened.'

As he approached the door of the apothecary shop, the door burst open. Sarah rushed out, into his arms.

'Oh, Levi! Levi, I've been so terrified! Where have you been? I was so afraid you were dead, that you'd tried to stop that awful mob or something, and I couldn't find you, and I was afraid to look for you, and you didn't come by or send any message, or . . . oh, Levi!'

He wrapped his arms around her and held her, feeling the uncontrolled trembling in her body.

'It's OK, Sarah. It's OK. You're OK. Nobody's going to hurt you.'

Slowly the trembling subsided, and Sarah's breathing became normal. She pushed back from Levi and brushed at the front of her dress.

'I'm – I'm sorry,' she said. 'You – you've made your wishes clear. I didn't mean to do that. I – I was just – I've been terribly frightened.'

'You got a right to be,' Levi assured her. 'Is your dad here?'

She nodded. 'He's inside. Him and three others. They're the only ones in town that seem to think this is all wrong. Nobody else cares, or dares to say anything. But they're only three. What can three men do?'

'We can't do much,' Sheriff Young entered the conversation. 'We can try to find survivors. I've wired the railroad, that they need to get some cars here to pick up survivors along the tracks. They can take them over to Evanston. There are Chinese there that they can probably find shelter with. That train is supposed to be on the way.'

Jonathan Miles stepped out the door.

'I thought I heard your voice, Sheriff. What can we do?'

'Well, I think we need to go as a group, so we have enough fire power to discourage any attacks on us, and see what's left of Hong Kong.'

'Not much,' Jonathan sighed. 'There were maybe fifty shacks that didn't get burned in the first go-round. They went back at sun-up and burned those. There's nothing left. Place looks like one o' them cyclone winds went through. Stuff strewn everywhere. Everything's busted. Dead bodies laying everywhere.'

'How many dead?'

'I have no idea. Somewhere between fifty and a hundred, I'd guess. Some of them were burned, so their remains are in with the ashes of their shacks. Some of those shacks had cellars, so there might even still be some hiding who survived. I doubt many though. There's been men going through the ashes looking for cellar doors to kill anyone left.'

'Still today?'

'Still today.'

Young shook his head. 'I thought it was sort of a mob hysteria yesterday. I thought by today they'd remember they're men.'

'I'm not sure they are,' Miles lamented. 'I'm not sure they are.'

'Well, we got to go do what we can.'

A man Levi did not know hurried up the sidewalk.

'Sheriff! Sheriff! There's a short train just pulled in. It's got Governor Warren's private car on it. The governor an' a dozen or two of his guards are here.'

'Well, that'll speed up the action o' gettin' the army at least,' Young said. 'Let's go meet the governor, and go on a tour o' what's left o' Hong Kong.'

'You go ahead,' Levi said. 'If you have the governor's guards, you won't need my gun. I've still got business to tend to.'

Fury stamped itself across Sarah's face. 'You're still going to keep pushing that thing?' she shouted. 'I can't believe you, Levi Hill! Don't you ever just give up?'

'Nope,' Levi said. His voice was harsher than he intended. 'I thought you'd figured that out.'

He whirled and stalked to his horse. Mounting he rode swiftly to the livery barn. He unsaddled, rubbed the horse down thoroughly, fed him some extra oats and hay, then walked into the street. He stopped abruptly.

'Enough is enough, Hill,' Randolph Dawson shouted. He held a double-barreled shotgun in the crook of his arm.

'Mr Dawson.' Levi greeted the distraught businessman. 'I'm not sure what you're talking about, but enough usually is enough.'

'I'm talking about this stupid investigation of my brother's murder,' Dawson raged. 'I just talked to Sarah, and she tells us that you're still pressing forward with it. Even now. Even after all that's gone on.'

'All this doesn't change what I was sent here to do,' Levi responded.

'It sure proves what we been tellin' you all along,' Dawson argued. 'It was just the first shot in this Chinese thing. And now the town has finally done the right thing and run them out. In the process of doing that, I'm confident we killed the one, or the ones, that shot Hiram. The matter is settled. His death is avenged. There is nothing more for you to do here.'

'How do you know you got the right one?'

'What difference does it make. We killed enough of those foreign pagans to avenge my brother. And we drove the rest of them out of town. And we got rid of that rat's nest they lived in. We cleansed the country of the blight that had come upon it with the arrival of those people.'

'You sure you didn't make a bigger blight on the country?'

'What do you mean?'

'I mean what you and the rest of this town did yesterday and last night will probably stand as one of the biggest blotches on the history of Wyoming Territory. When did you forget that you are men, and start acting like a mob of wild animals?'

'Animals? We did what we had to do, man! We did what needed to be done a long time ago. We tried, Hiram and me, to level the playing field, to give the white men in this town an even break, but the railroad even kept trying to stop us from that. What we did yesterday was a good and noble thing.'

'It was a weak and cowardly thing,' Levi argued. 'And it did nothing to change what I was sent here to do.'

'Somebody has to change what you were sent here to do. If the men I hired didn't take care of it, then I'll do it myself,' Dawson raged.

He grabbed his shotgun with both hands and lifted the barrels toward Levi. Levi's gun roared as the shotgun lifted. The shotgun continued to lift, up and to the side. Both barrels discharged at once, as Dawson's fingers spasmodically closed on them. The recoil of the shotgun sent it flying from his hands. He sprawled in the street, beside the gun.

Levi looked around quickly. The shots of his own and Dawson's guns had blended in with the random shooting that was going on all over town. Nobody even seemed to notice the drama of life and death that had played itself out. It was as if one more human life didn't even matter.

Levi felt himself shudder as he turned to notify the undertaker. He couldn't keep the bitterness from his voice as he said aloud, 'He'll prob'ly pick him up an' bury 'im. He's a white man.'

CHAPTER 13

'Why did you sic Dawson on me?'

Sarah backed away from Levi. Her eyes darted from his angry glare to the front door, then back again.

'What, what do you mean?'

'You told Dawson I was going to continue my investigation,' Levi accused.

'I . . . I . . . why would you say that?'

'It doesn't take a genius to figure that out. I told you I was going to go ahead with it. I didn't say anything to anyone else. Then less than two hours later Dawson braced me with a shotgun, to make me change my mind.'

'He . . . he did what?'

'He stuck a shotgun in my face,' Levi repeated. 'Because, he said, I was still going to keep on with my investigation. Now where, I ask you, might he have heard that? You were the only one I told.'

Sarah's face was so white her lips had even lost color.

'I . . . but . . . well, when you told me that, there were others here too. Sheriff Young was here. Mr Watkins was here. Walter Sanger was here. Walter is a businessman too. Maybe he told Randolph what you said.'

Doubt clouded Levi's certainty for a moment. He glared holes through the woman he had been convinced, a week ago, that he loved enough to give up his career for. Now he couldn't even believe her simple denial.

On the other hand, she hasn't really denied it, he realized silently.

He decided the direct approach would be most useful.

'So then tell me,' he demanded, 'did you tell Randolph Dawson what I said?'

'I – I – I don't know why you think it had to be me.'

'It probably didn't have to be you. That's why I'm asking. Was it you?'

Her lips clamped together. Her eyes flashed. She straightened up to her fiill height. She took a deep breath.

'Well, what if it was? I have the right to talk with whoever I want to. You have no right to try to tell me what to do or what to say. You maybe had a chance to have that right, but you made it very clear you didn't want it. Or at least not if you had to give up anything for it. So what right do you have stomping in here and demanding answers from me?'

'Having someone try to kill me because of you

124

might constitute that right,' he replied.

'He – he didn't really, did he? Try to kill you, I mean?'

'I don't think a Greener filled with buckshot was only meant to discourage me.'

'He actually shot at you with a shotgun?'

'He tried.'

'What do you mean?'

'I mean he wasn't quite fast enough.'

She stared at him in disbelief for a long moment.

'Are, are you saying you . . . he . . . you . . . you killed him?'

'That's exactly what I'm saying. He told me he was the one who hired the two gunmen to kill me. He told me he knew I was continuing the investigation into Hiram's murder. He told me to drop it and leave town. When I declined the invitation, he pulled up with that shotgun and tried to shoot me. I was a hair quicker, or I'd be laying in the street dead instead of him.'

'You . . . you killed him?'

'That's what I just said. Or you did. You sicced him on to me, didn't you?'

'Oh, but I didn't want anyone to get killed! There's been too much killing already. I didn't really even want all those awful Chinese to get killed. I just wanted to rid the town of them. I wanted them all chased away, not killed. And now Randolph too? Oh, poor Lily! Poor Addie! Now what are they going to do?'

'What are you going to do?' Levi pressed.

Tears welled in her eyes as she looked at him. 'What do you mean?'

'I mean, have enough people been killed yet for you to stop playing games?'

'I – I don't know what you're talking about.'

'I think you do. You've tried, since the first day I walked in here looking for balm for my hands, to talk me out of this investigation. You've tried everything from threats to . . . to . . . well, you know how far you've gone to get me to stop. There has to be a reason you're that dead set on stopping me. I think you could tell me what I need to know to wrap up this investigation. Why aren't you telling me?'

'I don't know what you're talking about,' she insisted.

'Who killed Hiram Dawson?' he demanded.

'What difference does it make?'

'It makes all the difference in the world.'

'Why?'

'Because a man was murdered.'

'Maybe he deserved to be murdered.'

'Did he?'

'What difference would it make to you. All you want to do is find somebody to be the scapegoat, so you can keep your almighty reputation going. It doesn't matter to you how many other people are killed, does it? It doesn't matter to you how many reputations are ruined, does it? It doesn't matter to you how many good people's lives are destroyed, does it? All that matters to you is that you solve your precious case. Then you can ride off into the sunset the bigger-than-life legend of Wyoming. That's what really matters, isn't it?'

'What really matters is justice. If someone's been killed, then the killer needs to be brought to justice.'

'Really? Really? Is that what really matters to you? Then you run right out there and take a walk down through Hong Kong, and you find out who murdered all those Chinese whose bodies are lying in the street. If you want justice so bad, go get it! There's enough murders there to keep you busy for the rest of your stupid life, and you can get off of this one!'

'Why?'

'What do you mean, "Why?" '

'Why do you want me off this one so badly?'

'Stop coming back to that all the time! Can't you even think about anything else?'

'No. Not right now. This is the one I'm trying to solve.'

'Well stop trying to solve it! How many times do I have to tell you that?'

'What is there you don't want me finding out? Did you kill him?'

Sarah gasped. Her eyes widened. The color drained from her face again. He thought she was going to faint for a moment.

'Why on earth would you say that?'

'Because I can't figure out any other reason you'd be so dead set on keeping me from finding out who did it.'

'Well, you can rest your mind on that one,

mister detective! I certainly did not kill him, and I did not have anything to do with his death. There. Are you happy?'

Levi studied her face for a long moment. 'OK. I guess I believe that. So who did?'

'We're back to that, huh?'

'We're back to that. Who did it?'

'Levi, if you knew who Hiram Dawson really was . . . If you knew what Hiram Dawson really was . . . Levi, I'm just telling you, drop it. Leave it. Forget it. Ride away. There isn't anything for you here. Not any more, anyway. Go away. Just leave us all alone.'

'And if I don't?'

'If you don't, then I guess you'll just have to do what you have to do. It won't matter to you if you destroy Lily and Addle both, will it?'

'Why would finding out who murdered their father destroy them?'

'Never mind. There's no point in even trying to talk to you. Just go. Get out of my store. Go away. I don't want to talk to you any more. I don't want to see you any more. Just get out of my life!'

By the time she finished, she was screaming at the top of her voice, pushing him toward the front door. He decided he had pushed her as far as he could. There was nothing more to gain here.

As he walked out and she slammed the door behind him, a yawning cavern of grief opened up within him, threatening to consume him, to devour him in its emptiness.

'So much for that dream,' he muttered, as he stalked down the street.

CHAPTER 14

'Still no sign of the army?'

Watkins looked back and forth, out the window of his office.

'Nope. They're supposed to be on the way.'

'They were supposed to be on the way three days ago,' Levi reminded him.

'Tell me about it!'

'It's settled down some.'

'Only because they can't find any more Chinese to kill.'

'At least the railroad did something right. Sending that train to pick up all the survivors got 'em over to Evanston.'

'There wouldn't have been any, except for you.'

'What do you mean?'

'You having Tang Lu warn everyone to hightail it outa there prob'ly saved two or three hundred lives.'

'I'm glad of that, at least.'

'I didn't think they'd go as far as they did.'

'Who?'

'The mobs. People. I didn't think they'd ever do something that bad. I know these people! I see 'em in church. I do business with 'em. I drink with 'em, an' play cards with 'em. I thought I knew 'em. Then they just all went nuts. I don't understand it.'

'Hate.'

'Yeah, there's a lot of that.'

'I mean it's hate. Hate is a real thing. It's a form of evil. It's a lever that evil uses to get hold of people, and twist them. Once anyone gives in and lets himself hate, he's capable of anything. As long as you fight the urge to hate, you stay human. But once you stop fighting, once you give in and let yourself hate, then it gets ahold of you inside, and warps and twists who you are and what you are, and you're capable of doing the worst things in the world.'

Watkins considered Levi's words for a long while in silence. Eventually he sighed heavily.

'Yeah, maybe you're right. I seen their faces. Some o' the miners didn't surprise me that much. I didn't really know 'em. Some of 'em was hard-cases to start with. But men I knowed. Men I liked. I seen their faces. I seen 'em when someone was shootin' Chinese, or hackin' at 'em, or runnin' a pick into their head after they was already dead. It was like lookin' into the face o' devils. They was the faces o' fiends. Plumb evil. Such evil it made my blood run cold. Just laughin' an' cheerin' like they was watchin' someone ridin' a tough bronc. Only they was killin' folks.'

'I 'spect they'd convinced themselves for a while

that Chinese wasn't really folks,' Levi offered. 'Once they gave in to the hate, they started thinking of 'em as some kind o' animal. Like rats or coyotes or somethin', that needed killed.'

'But they ain't.'

'No. They ain't. They're just as human as we are.'

'An' we killed 'em.'

'We?'

'Whites. That's us. I guess that makes me as guilty as the ones that pulled the triggers. Maybe, if I'd tried harder, I could've stopped 'em.'

'No. You'd only have gotten yourself killed too.'

'Maybe. Maybe that'd be better. Then I'd have done all I could. Then I wouldn't sit here feelin' guilty as sin.'

'Well, if that's the case, I'm just as guilty,' Levi countered. 'I rode out of town, when I saw it starting. I rode to Green River to try to get help, instead of standing at one of the bridges to keep the mobs from crossing over.'

'Yeah, but that made sense,' Watkins argued. 'I didn't even do that. I just argued with 'em, and tried to talk sense into 'em. I'd as well talked to the wind.'

'So we both did the best thing we could think of,' Levi suggested. 'There's no sense second-guessing ourselves now.'

'I s'pose not. Sure wish the army'd get here. The streets aren't even safe for me, with the mobs still hangin' around, drinkin' an' carousin'. Every decent woman in town's forted up at home somewhere, 'cause she don't dare be seen on the street.

133

I never understood what "mob rule" meant. Now I do. I hope I never see it again.'

'You and me both,' Levi agreed. 'I see some of the boys from the HH rode in.'

'Yeah. Three or four of the ranches sent men in. They're all hangin' around the Pioneer. They'll help restore order if we have to use 'em, but there ain't enough of 'em.'

'They came to help?'

Watkins nodded. 'Yeah. They all did. Heard what was goin' on. Sent as many hands as they could spare. Offered 'em to me, if I wanted to deputize 'em. I told 'em only Young could do that, so we're waitin' for him to show up again.'

'Think he will?'

Watkins snorted. 'Not if he's got any sense. Not till the army gets here.'

'I was surprised the governor did.'

Watkins snorted again. 'Yeah! Big deal! Strutted around town with his bodyguards. Strutted through what's left o' Hong Kong, just to show everyone he ain't scared. Then he went back to that private car on the railroad track, surrounded by his guards, armed to the teeth, to wait for the anny. Fat lot o' good he did.'

'Not much else he could do.'

'Naw, I s'pose not.'

'Well, I'm gonna wander back over to Ma Corder's. Every time I talk to somebody, I find out something more about Dawsons. Sooner or later I'll find the piece that makes the whole puzzle make sense.'

'You still don't think it was the Chinese?'

'Not for a minute. I never did, really. But since everything busted loose anyway, there's no more reason for anyone to not want me to find out it was. It wouldn't hurt a thing, now, to find out which Chinese it was, even. If the Chinese did it. But I'm still running into just as much resistance as I was. It seems like half the town's dead set on me not finding out who killed him.'

'Yeah, well, maybe half the town's right.'

'You too?'

Watkins shrugged without answering. Levi studied him for a long moment, then walked out.

He was half way to Ma Corder's boarding-house when a young man stepped into the street facing him.

'Howdy, Hill.'

'I guess you have the advantage,' Levi responded. 'I think I saw you at the HH, but I don't know your name.'

'Kendrick. Perry Kendrick. Yeah, I ride for Haines.'

'You part of the boys Hank sent in to help out.'

'Yup. That ain't got nothin' to do with my business with you, though.'

'Oh? And what business do you have with me?'

'Call it off.'

'Call what off?'

'This investigation. The Dawson thing. Drop it.'

'Why?'

' 'Cause it's just gonna get too many people hurt too bad.'

'Like who?'

'Like his girls.'

'Lily and Adelia?'

'That's them.'

'Why would my investigation hurt them?'

'It already is. It's tearin' 'em to pieces. Let it drop.'

'What's your interest in it?'

'I'm, I mean, that is, well, Lily, she's my intended.'

'You're courting Lily?'

'That's right. We aim to get married. The sooner you drop this thing an' get lost, the quicker we can do that.'

'Now why would my investigation have anything to do with your marrying Lily?'

'It just does. She won't marry me till that's all settled, an' it ain't gonna be settled till you leave town. So I'm here to tell you to leave town.'

'And if I don't?'

'Then I'll have to make ya.'

'And how do you intend to do that?'

'I'll . . . I'll kill you if I have to, to make you leave her alone.'

'Perry, I'm an officer of the law. If you threaten me, or try to kill me, then one of two things is going to happen. The first, and the most likely, is that I'm going to have to kill you. You aren't a gunman, Perry. I've been a gunman all my life. You don't have any more chance against me than a kid with a slingshot. And if I don't kill you, I'll have to arrest you for trying to kill an officer of the law.'

'Don't matter none. If you ain't gonna leave Lily alone an' ride out, then go for your gun.'

Levi sighed heavily. He looked at the fuzz on Perry's lip, where he was obviously trying his best to grow a mustache.

'How old are you, boy?'

'Nineteen.'

'Nineteen years old, and can't wait to die.'

'I don't wanta die. I just ain't gonna let you harass Lily no more. I wanta marry her. Give her the kinda life she shoulda had to start with. But you gotta get outa town for it to happen.'

'Why didn't she have that kind of life to start with?'

' 'Cause she . . . 'cause .. it don't make no difference. You gonna get outa town, or you gonna go for your gun?'

Levi eyed the lad carefully. He was poised on the balls of his feet. His hand was suspended just over the butt of his gun. The gun was too high on his hip for a very fast draw. It was positioned in the usual manner of a working cowboy, accessible for snakes or angry animals, not intended for gunfights. He was a scared but very determined kid, not a gunman. Still, more than one experienced gunman had been slain by just such a scared kid.

He started walking toward Perry. As he did, he said, 'You're not a gunman, Perry. Have you ever killed a man? Do you think you can look a man in the face, and put a bullet into him?'

As Perry hesitated, Levi continued to walk. He

walked right up to him. Perry didn't know how to respond. He never saw it coming. As Levi stepped up in front of him, his hand swept his .45 from its holster. In one smooth motion, more swift than Perry's best reaction on his very finest day, Levi's gun continued upward. It crashed into the side of Perry's head with a sickening thud. The young cowboy collapsed into the street.

Levi holstered his gun. He sighed again. He scooped Perry's undrawn pistol from its holster, and tucked it into the waistband of his trousers. He grabbed the cowpoke's hands, lifting the unconscious lad into a sitting position. His head lolled over to one side.

Pulling the hands he gripped over his shoulder and holding them in the middle of his back, Levi put his shoulder into the man's stomach. Then he straightened, lifting him, draping him across his shoulder. He walked to the Pioneer saloon.

Pushing his way through the front door, Levi spotted Beam and three of the HH hands, sitting at a table. He walked over and dumped Perry unceremoniously on to the sawdust-covered floor.

'Here's your hand, Beam,' he said, fighting to keep his breathing and speech from betraying any exertion. 'He tried to make me draw on 'im.'

'He seems to be breathin',' Beam responded.

'I just rapped him up side the head,' Levi responded. 'I ain't in the habit o' killin' kids.'

'Well, thanks for that,' Beam responded.

'Why's he so all-fired anxious for me to leave town?' Levi demanded.

'That ain't for me to say,' Beam replied. He made no effort to indicate he didn't know. He simply made it crystal clear that Levi would learn nothing from him. 'I tried to tell you that at the ranch, if you remember.'

Perry groaned and stirred. Levi looked around the table, meeting the hard steel of the eyes that glared back at him.

'Well, you'd as well know, I'll find out, sooner or later.'

'Don't bet on it,' Beam responded. 'But you do what you gotta do.'

That's exactly what Levi intended to do.

CHAPTER 15

Mob rule in Rock Springs was drawing to a close. Rampant bloodlust was, for the moment at least, sated. The army had arrived. They bivouacked outside of town, upstream, along Bitter Creek. That gave them access to the water of the creek above where it was hopelessly polluted with the dead bodies still reeking within it.

Burial parties had begun the grisly work of digging a mass grave, and transporting bloated bodies of dead Chinese to it. Officers consulted with Watkins and Sheriff Joe Young for patrolling the streets of Rock Springs. Martial law would be the order of the day at daybreak.

Already the presence of the army had changed the climate of the town. Mobs that had roamed the streets, carousing and gloating since the not, were mostly gone now. In their wake, the town looked like a great storm had left it crippled and littered. No building on Front Street had escaped bullet holes, fired at random. Windows were shattered. A couple stores, left unguarded, had been looted. All

141

the rest had received random damage. Now the streets were empty and silent.

Levi walked the silence of the empty streets, pondering his next move. He decided he had to try once more to talk with Hiram Dawson's daughters. Maybe if he talked with the younger one alone, she would be more willing to tell him something. She obviously knew something. Several times, when he was talking with the two sisters together, the younger one had started to say something, and been cut off abruptly by her older sister. Like the rest of the town, it seemed, they knew a lot more than they were willing to tell Levi.

Why? It still made no sense to him. They, of all people, should want to learn the truth of their father's murder. Yet they seemed at the center of every effort to force him to abandon his investigation.

It was the silence of the now empty streets that saved his life. He heard the barrel of a rifle rub against the boards on the corner of a building. A hammer clicked softly to cocked position. If there had been any traffic at all on those littered streets, he would never have heard it.

But he heard it. His finely honed instincts sent him in an instant dive to the ground, even as the rifle-shot barked into the silence of the dusk. The bullet struck the building he had been in front of with a flat *thwack*. He rolled, coming to his feet, gun in hand. He fired three times, swiftly, into the alleyway between two stores. It was from there he had seen the flash of fire, from the corner of his eye, as he dived.

His frustration and anger boiled over. Throwing caution to the winds, he sprinted directly to the gap between stores. As he plunged into the narrow opening, he saw a figure just ducking out from the back end of the narrow opening. He dashed the length of the alley, not even protecting himself from the danger of ambush.

Lunging into the open, he spotted his quarry less than twenty yards in front of him. He holstered his gun as he ran, quickly closing the distance between them. He instinctively hooked the strap over his gun, which would keep it in its holster, then he dived at the legs of the fleeing assailant.

His shoulder barreled into the lower legs of the running sniper. The would-be killer flopped to the ground hard, driving the air from hammered lungs with an audible gush.

Levi allowed the fiigitive no time to recover. He grabbed the rifle, wrenching it from a surprisingly weak grip, and throwing it aside. He jerked the figure over facc up, jumped astraddle the supine form, and drove his fist downward.

With a super-human effort he stopped the fist before it contacted the fragile-looking face of a young woman.

'Lily!' he exclaimed. 'What in the Sam Hill do you think you're doing?'

Lily Dawson's wide eyes looked back at him in abject terror. 'Please, don't hit me!' she said. Her voice was tiny, plaintive.

'You tried to kill me!' Levi accused. 'Why did you try to kill me?'

'Please don't hit me!' Lily pleaded again. 'Oh, please! Just kill me. Just kill me and say you were shooting back at me.'

'Why would I kill you?'

She didn't answer. The terror slowly left her eyes. In its wake, her eyes turned flat and empty. Her body went totally limp.

'You'd just as well,' she said.

'Why? I've been given the run-around on this deal long enough. You're out of time. Tell me why!'

He thought she was going to cry. Then he realized the grief and pain in her eyes was too deep for tears. Sympathy washed through him, overwhelming every other emotion. He had no idea why, but the abject level of her misery rinsed his anger away. He fought the urge to lift her to her feet and fold her into a protective embrace.

He got to his feet. He took her hand.

'Here. Let me help you up.' He pulled her to her feet. 'Come on,' he ordered. His voice was harsh, brusque, to hide the emotions he struggled with. 'We're going over to J.C. Watkins's ofice, and you're going to answer a lot of questions.'

He scooped up her rifle from where he had flung it. He kept her wrist firmly in the grip of his left hand. He unfastened the strap from his pistol again. He marched her directly to Watkins's office.

The office was empty, but open. He shoved Lily toward a chair.

'Sit!' he barked.

Meekly, she obeyed. She folded her hands in her lap and stared at them. She said nothing.

Levi lifted one leg across a corner of Watkins's desk, half-sitting on its corner.

'Talk!' he demanded.

For nearly a full minute there was no response. Then in a small voice, flat and expressionless, fraught with resignation, Lily responded.

'What do you want to know?'

'Everything. Who killed your father?'

Without hesitation she said, 'I did.'

Levi felt as if a horse had just kicked him in the gut. He couldn't find words to respond. He tried to swallow, but a lump in his throat prevented it. He tried to speak, but his mouth was suddenly too dry. He took a deep breath. All the evidence he had missed swept across his memory in a parade of clues he had refused to recognize. The location of the murder, the ties of Lily to every one who had impeded the investigation, the hints that Sarah had unwittingly offered. He felt suddenly as stupid and inept as he had ever felt in his life. With an effort he found his voice.

'Suppose you start at the beginning, and tell me the whole story.'

'All of it?'

'Every bit of it.'

A dry sob racked her spare frame. Emotion returned to her voice. 'Do – do I have to tell you everything? All . . . all the details?'

'Every detail,' Levi demanded. 'I got to make a

decision what to do about you. I can't make a decision without all the facts. I don't know what the story is, but I got to know it all.'

Another period of profound silence followed. When she started speaking it was as if a dam had suddenly burst, and she couldn't wait until all its putrid back-up was drained from her.

'It started after Mama died,' she began. Her voice was still flat, toneless. But there was the urgency of some pressure behind it. Some pressure within her forced long-pent secrets into the open. 'I was thirteen. I was old for my age, I guess. At least everyone said I looked like a woman already. For quite a while we had a hard time without Mama. Daddy cried every night. I did the cooking and kept the house. I knew how. Mama had taught me really good. After while, Daddy didn't cry so much. But he was so sad all the time.

'Then he started being . . . different with me. He started putting his arms around me a lot. He hadn't ever done that very much. He started patting me, on . . . on my bottom, as he walked past me. Then sometimes I'd wake up at night, and he'd be lying beside me in bed. Sometimes he'd be touching me, different places.

'It seemed like every day he'd touch me more. Then he started to kiss me, sometimes. He'd kiss me on the side of my neck, or on my cheek. Then he started kissing me on my lips. It didn't seem really right, but it didn't seem bad or anything. Then he started telling me how hard it was for him to be alone, without a wife. He told me how much

I reminded him of Mama. He told me how much Mama would want me to take care of him.

'Then he started touching me in places I knew he shouldn't. One night he took my nightshirt off of me, and started touching me all over. Then I noticed he didn't have any clothes on either. He told me a man really has to have a woman, but he couldn't be going down to the saloon to those women who are there, because they have all sorts of diseases. He said with Mama gone, I needed to be his woman now.'

Levi felt as if he had to speak or explode. 'How old were you?'

'I was fourteen then. He started, started, using me, like I was his wife.'

'At fourteen?'

She nodded, staring at her hands. 'I was really big for my age. I was pretty much a woman. At first it hurt, but he tried to be really careful. After while, it started feeling good. I knew it was wrong, but he told me it was my duty. I wanted to be a good daughter.'

'How long did that go on?'

'Ever since. It never stopped.'

'For how long?'

'I'm eighteen now. Four years.'

'And you didn't ever, I mean, you weren't ever. . . ?'

'In a family way?'

'Yeah.'

'Yes. Once. Daddy took me to Dr Zastrow. He did something to me that made me hurt really,

really bad. And I bled an awful lot. After that Dr Zastrow told me that he'd had a talk with my father, and if he ever tried to do things to me again to come and tell him. He said Daddy could go to jail for doing that to his daughter.'

'But he didn't quit.'

'He did for a while. Three or four months. Then he started again.'

'And you didn't tell the doctor?'

She shook her head. 'I was afraid. I didn't want Daddy to go to jail.'

'Why didn't you just tell him no?'

She sighed as if the weight of the world was on her shoulders.

'Because I knew Daddy really needed a woman. Adelia is only a couple years younger than me. I knew if I didn't let him use me, he would probably start using her instead. I didn't want that to happen to her.'

'So you let him just keep using you, to protect her.'

She nodded, but did not speak.

After a long silence he prodded her again. 'Then what happened?'

Another dry sob racked her body. She fought for control. When she was able, she continued: 'Then I woke up one night, and I was really thirsty. I went out to the kitchen to get a drink from the water bucket. When I went by Addie's room, I saw Daddy in there with her. He was telling her the same things he told me, when he started doing it to me.'

Levi could think of nothing to say, so he said nothing.

After a long pause, Lily continued, 'I knew I had to do something. I couldn't let him do all those things to her too. I got his shotgun the next day. I waited for him to come home from the store. He came home, and went out to the shed to take care of the cow. When he was coming back in, I stepped outside the back door and shot him. I didn't even say anything. I don't think he even saw me, before I shot. He wasn't looking at me. And I didn't feel anything. I thought I'd feel really, really bad, but I don't. I just didn't feel anything. But at least he isn't ever going to do to Addie what he did to me!'

After he could find his voice, Levi asked, 'Does Perry know all that?'

She nodded without looking up. 'I had to tell him, when he asked me to marry him. I think he was going to kill Daddy. That's another reason I did it. I didn't want him to go to jail for doing something that I needed to do.'

After another long silence, he asked, 'Do other people know?'

She shook her head quickly, emphatically. 'The rest of the people on the ranch where Perry works know that Daddy was really mean to me. Perry told them that Daddy beat both of us girls all the time. He wouldn't tell them all the things that would, would ruin my reputation that much. That's why they didn't want you to investigate. They knew you'd find out he was mean, and figure out that maybe I was the one that killed him.'

'And the good doctor, who knew the truth,

wouldn't trust me with the information,' Levi breathed. 'But he sure tried to persuade me to leave town.'

'Uncle Randolph knew, too, I think,' Lily continued. 'I heard him telling Daddy once that if the family ever found out something like that, they could kiss that whole inheritance goodbye. I don't know what inheritance that is, but he didn't seem to care about me. He just cared about it.'

Silence filled the small office. It pressed around them, stifling the air. It became deep and profound, as if it would be some great sin to break it. It held them in its iron grip. Both of them opened their mouths several times, but the oppressive silence bade them close them again.

In that heavy silence, Levi's mind cast about desperately for solutions that would not destroy the fragile, abused life before him. He couldn't think of a one.

CHAPTER 16

Boots clumped heavily on the board sidewalk. The office door burst open. J. C. Watkins stepped inside, taking off his hat as he entered.

He stopped in his tracks. Levi still half-sat on the corner of the desk. Lily huddled in the chair, hands folded in her lap. Neither looked up as Watkins entered.

Watkins swore explosively. He glared at Levi.

'So you figgered it out.'

Levi looked up slowly. The deputy stood just inside the door, hat in hand. His head was thrust forward. His mustache bristled. His eyes burned holes at Levi.

Levi sighed. 'She told me.'

'I tried to kill him,' Lily said softly.

Watkins's glare whipped around to burn at Lily. 'You what?'

'She took a pot shot at me,' Levi affirmed.

'Well ain't that all the luck,' Watkins growled. 'She missed.'

'Thanks a lot,' Levi shot back.

'So I s'pose she spilled the whole pot o' beans.'

'She told me,' Levi repeated.

'So now what? Why couldn't ya just leave well enough alone? How many lives you gonna have to ruin, just so you can have your almighty justice?'

'Justice still has to be done.' Levi sighed.

Watkins snorted. 'Yeah! Justice! Two purty little girls been through stuff nobody oughta never have to deal with. But they survived it. Lily's got a chanct at a decent life with that cowboy. Now you gotta come in an' use your almighty justice to destroy both of 'em. Do you know what it'll do to 'em in this country if word o' what's gone on ever gets out? They won't be able to hold up their head in public the rest o' their lives. An' it ain't no fault o' theirn.'

'What choice is there?' Levi lamented.

'Same choice there's always been. Get your self-righteous behind outa this town an' let things stand like they was afore you come.'

'But a murder's been committed,' Levi protested. 'That can't be ignored. Not if there's any rule of law at all.'

Watkins snorted again. 'There's been a whole lot o' murders around here lately,' he reminded. 'Or don't you count all them Chinese gettin' tossed in a big hole in the ground as murders? Who d'ya think's ever gonna get held responsible for them? Where's your precious justice there?'

'That's different. I have no control over that. I have no responsibility over that.'

'Then what makes you think you do over this?'

'It's what I was sent to deal with. It's what Pinkerton accepted a contract to find out.'

'Why?'

'Why what?'

'Why's Pinkerton interested? It ain't like Dawson was some big-wig or somethin'.'

Levi looked back and forth from Watkins to Lily for a long while. He sighed heavily, for what seemed like the tenth time in the past five minutes.

'Dawson's parents live back East. They're well to do. Pretty big estate, I think. Three or four hundred thousand dollars. They're both about to die. They're wanting to settle their estate. Leave it to their family. The two boys are their only kids. Were their only kids. Now it's just Lily and Adelia.'

'So they stand to heir a big bunch o' money?'

'Maybe. That's why they hired Pinkerton. They wanted to be sure the ones they willed the estate to deserved to have that kind of money. They got word of Hiram's murder. They were worried that maybe Randolph was behind it. They said they could never leave that kind of estate to a murderer.'

The suffocating weight of silence swept back down and enveloped the small office. Each was lost in a world of tumbling thoughts. It was Watkins who broke it.

'Then, when you file your report, an' Lily's charged with murder, it'll wipe her plumb outa that will.'

Levi nodded. 'I imagine it will.'

'So she gets . . . gets . . . used like that by her own

pa, then she gets charged with murderin' 'im, then she gets done outa her inheritance too. That's what you call justice?'

'The law's the law,' Levi defended.

Watkins snorted so loud his bushy mustache fluttered. He gave no other answer. He simply wheeled and stalked out of the office, slamming the door behind him.

Levi studied Lily for a long while in silence. Several times he started to say something, then stopped. Eventually he asked, 'Did Sarah know?'

Lily nodded silently.

'So her pretendin' to be in love with me was just that. Pretendin'. Just to get me to leave town, even if she had to leave with me.'

Lily looked up at him. The depth of emptiness in her eyes wrenched him.

'At first, maybe. Then she really did fall in love with you. No, I think she fell in love with you first. She fell in love with you that very first day you went in there to get that salve for your hands. Then she got the idea of using it to get you to leave town with her. She hates it here. If you'd have done it, she could have gotten away from here, she'd have had you, and she'd have saved Addle and me from all this. She really thought it was the perfect plan.'

Levi swallowed hard. 'Love just don't manipulate like that.'

'She really does love you,' Lily pleaded.

Levi's voice was harsher than he intended. 'That's over. I just got to figure out what to do with you.'

Lily didn't answer. Her eyes dropped to her hands again. After another long silence, Levi said:

'Well, I don't see any choice. I have to take you over to Green River.'

'You're arresting me?'

'I don't have any choice.'

'Then what?'

'Then they'll have a hearing before a judge, when he comes through. I imagine, when everybody testifies, he'll rule that you were justified in shooting your father. Then you'll be released, but justice will be satisfied.'

'But what about Addle and me?'

'What do you mean?'

'After everything that's happened is gossiped all over the country, we'll be thought of as no different from the whores down at the saloon. No decent man will ever consider courting either one of us. And we won't even have that inheritance to live on. What will we do? We won't even be able to run the store, because nobody would do business with us.'

Silence draped a curtain of despair over the room, as Levi cast about in his mind for a better solution. He simply couldn't find one.

'It's dark already,' he said. 'We best get going.'

Lily nodded meekly and rose. She shuffled to the door, opened it, and stepped out, with Levi close behind her. She stopped so abruptly Levi bumped into her before he could stop.

Ranged before the door were half a dozen men. J.C. Watkins, in the center of the group, held the

reins of Buck, Levi's horse. Lined up to either side
of him were Perry Kendrick and four of the hands
from the HH. Three of them carried double-
barreled shotguns.

'What are you doing?' Levi demanded.

'Lily, step away,' Perry said. 'Move over there,
away from Hill.'

'What are you doing?' Levi demanded again.

Watkins's scowl was so deep his hair and
eyebrows looked as if they were going to meet. His
eyes peered intently through them at Levi.

'Well, we been talkin',' he announced. 'About
justice.'

'Justice?'

'Justice. That's what you want, ain't it?'

'Of course.'

'Well, then give a listen, an' think about this. If
you go an' arrest this little of girl, she's gonna have
to stand trial. On account o' everybody knowin'
that her pa abused her an' her little sister, beat on
'em like you wouldn't beat on a horse, made 'em
be plumb slaves, livin' in fear o' their lives and all,
that when she up an' shot 'im she wasn't doin'
nothin' but defendin' herself an' her sister.'

Levi considered correcting the lawman, then
thought better of it. Even if Watkins knew the true
story, there was no need for the riders from the
HH to know. He held his silence while Watkins
continued:

'That there's self-defense. That there ain't no
different than you shootin' Randolph. Now you
wouldn't think it justice if you was hauled off to

court for shootin' Randolph, would you?'

'Why would I be?'

'Oh, maybe because them high-falutin relations of his decided to hire Pinkerton to find out who shot their other boy. Then justice would require you to be arrested an' stand trial for that, wouldn't it?'

'Well, if that happened, then I suppose maybe. But it would be ruled self-defense.'

'So you're sayin' there'd be no sense in doin' it?'

'Of course.'

'Then how's Lily's case any different from yourn?'

Levi studied each of the group in turn. Their faces were set in iron determination. He turned his attention back to Watkins.

'So what are you saying?'

'We're saying that now you know the facts, it's time to call your job done here. It seems the most likely thing that both Hiram an' Randolph Dawson were killed by persons unknown, most likely Chinese, for their helpin' out the white miners. In all the mess the riots caused, there ain't no way to ever find out nothin' beyond that. That way you don't have to stand trial for shootin' Randolph, an' Lily don't have to stand trial for shootin' Hiram. Case closed.'

'And if I refuse to go along with that?'

'Well, me'n these boys aim to make sure that don't happen. We sorta took the liberty o' packin' up all your stuff from over at Ma Corder's. It ain't maybe packed just like you'da done, but it's all there. We got your horse from the livery barn. It seems like justice is about to be done here. Assumin' you agree to it, that is.'

'What if I agree to it, then ride to Green River and file charges?'

'You won't.'

'Why not?'

' 'Cause you're Levi Hill. Everybody knows Levi Hill ain't never broke his word in his life. If you say agree to the deal, you'll live by it.'

'It's still not the truth.'

'No. No it ain't. But it's justice. I guess sometimes justice needs to be a lie.'

'Justice is a lie?'

'Or a lie is justice. This time, anyhow.'

Levi looked over at Lily. She huddled against the front wall of Watkins's office. She looked as abject and forlorn as anyone Levi had ever seen. He turned back to the group ranged in front of him.

'Perry, get over there and take care of your woman. She needs you.'

Perry stared uncomprehendingly for an instant. Then a smile slowly spread across his face. He rushed over to Lily, sweeping her into the circle of his arms, holding her close, murmuring into her hair.

Levi stepped forward and took Buck's reins from Watkins. He turned back to Perry and Lily. 'ferry, you take good care of her. Don't you ever let anyone hurt her again.'

'I won't,' Perry promised.

'And her sister too. They'll be coming into an

158

awfiilly big chunk of money one of these days. You'll have to be the one to look out for Adelia too. You make sure any guy that sets his hat for her is doing it for her, not for the money she'll have.'

He stepped into the saddle and touched the spurs to Buck's sides. He didn't look back as he trotted out of a town he never wanted to see again.